Love-Lies-Bleeding

Barbara Haworth-Attard

Cover illustration by Melissa Joseph-Mirani

ROUSSAN
PUBLISHERS INC.
Specializing in YA and fiction for pre-teens

THE CANADA COUNCIL | LE CONSEIL DES ARTS
FOR THE ARTS | DU CANADA
SINCE 1957 | DEPUIS 1957

We acknowledge the support of the Canada
Council for the Arts for our publishing program.

We acknowledge the financial support of the Government
of Canada through the Book Publishing Industry
Development Program for our publishing activities.

http://www.roussan.com

Copyright ©1999 by Barbara Haworth-Attard

National Library of Canada
Bibliothèque nationale du Québec

Canadian Cataloguing in Publication Data
Haworth-Attard, Barbara, 1953-
Love, lies, bleeding
(On time's wing)

ISBN 1-896184-60-x

1.World War, 1939-1945-Canada-Juvenile fiction.

I. Title. II. Series.

PS8565.A865L69 1999   jC813'.54   C99-900921-4
PZ7.H31364Lo 1999

Cover design by Dan Clark
Interior design by Jean Shepherd
Amaranthus Caudatus graphic by Donald Lemieux

Stone Print

Published simultaneously in Canada and the United States of America
Printed in Canada

2 3 4 5 6 7 8 9 AGMV-MRQ 7 6 5 4 3 2 1 0 9

For my brothers, Jim, David, Doug and Ken

Special thanks to my father's sister, Mildred Christopher, for sharing her recollections of home-front life during 1943. My mother, Trudy Haworth, also shared her memories though, sadly, died before she saw the book completed.

Amaranthus caudatus (love-lies-bleeding): A tropical plant bearing spectacular crimson tassels of tiny blooms which reach lengths of 18 inches.

Amaranth: an imaginary flower that never dies.

September 12, 1944

"For such a small country in population to be doing such a big job over here—I think the Canadians have done their part well."

Lawrence Haworth

After my dad died in 1994, we discovered a suitcase in the basement that contained his war memorabilia, including letters he wrote home to his parents in Richmond Hill, Ontario, during his six years overseas. Excerpts from these letters are woven throughout this story to give the reader an authentic sense of what it felt like to be fighting so far from home. Though restricted by censorship, the letters chronicled the life of an ordinary soldier in World War II: from training in England to his participation in various theatres of war, including Sicily, Italy, France, Belgium, Holland and, finally, Germany itself.

They told of terrible destruction, atrocities and the stink of death. They spoke of the loneliness that occasionally overwhelmed him, the low morale of the soldiers and the enduring hope for peace and a return home. They also stated over and over his conviction that he had to be there. This ordinary man doing extraordinary things became my father.

Another battle was being waged at the same time with the same elements involved—loneliness, low morale and the hope for peace—but this one was being waged at home. Mothers, sisters, wives, husbands, fathers, and friends were sending their loved ones overseas, not knowing if they would ever return. I look at my own sons, aged twenty-one and seventeen, and I wonder: could I do it? Could I part with them, not knowing if I'd ever see them again? It defies my imagination.

Barbara Haworth-Attard

Autumn 1943

Dear Mother and Dad and All,

We're supposed to be volunteers in the Canadian Army and that's that. To tell you the truth I'm fed up with this army and there are many like me.

From,
Your son

Sunday, September 12, 1943

I, Roberta Harrison, have to keep a diary and it's all the fault of the Worm of Jealousy.

Monday, September 13, 1943

I first heard about the Worm of Jealousy in Sunday school. Rev. Goddard said when you want something someone else has, and that want gives you a niggling feeling in the stomach, it is the Worm of Jealousy turning. Nancy Goddard whispered in my ear that the Worm of Jealousy is a gas bubble trying to get out. Only she didn't say gas bubble, she said f—t. For a minister's daughter, Nancy is *appallingly* rude. I don't imagine the Worm of Jealousy bothers her much.

Tuesday, September 14, 1943

I don't even know how to write a diary. I know some diaries start off with *Dear Diary*, but that's too much like letter writing and I already have to write letters every Sunday afternoon to my brother Alex and my uncle Billy who are over at the war. I don't even have a proper diary, just an old math notebook that I tore the used pages from, so who cares if I write improper in my improper diary. Oh no! Now the back pages are falling out. *Misery!* (I've decided to keep a list of my most favourite words to show Alex when he comes home.)

Wednesday, September 15, 1943

Here is how the Worm of Jealousy made me keep a diary: My best friend, Betty, had her fourteenth birthday party. She is a year older than me, but still in Grade Eight because she was held back a year due to her having scarlet fever when she was little. Betty says I am to make it crystal clear to everyone this is why she is in Grade Eight—not because she's dumb like Nancy Goddard says. There were four girls at the party; Lydia (Betty's other best friend), Diane (Betty's cousin), me and, of course, Betty. The mothers were invited to tea at the same time. Mother complained about not having time to go to tea parties, but she put on her Sunday skirt and blouse anyway. I was very proud to show Mother the Double Doors at the entrance to Betty's house. Dad says they're built like that to let wide people through, but I told him Double Doors are the height of elegance. Betty's family has Double Doors because her father is the bank manager of the Canadian Bank of Commerce on Dundas Street downtown.

Before ringing the bell at Betty's, Mother's hand went to her hair and I know just how she felt. I always check that my buttons are done up right on my sweater when I stand in front of Betty's Double Doors.

Inside Betty's house I took a deep breath because it smells like flowers. Our house smells like fried onions and my brothers' dirty feet. Mother sat on the sofa with the other ladies and I sat on the floor. Betty began opening her presents and that is when the Worm of Jealousy first stirred. She got an adorable pale blue sweater, a silver locket on a chain (the Worm twisted so hard at that necklace my stomach hurt), perfume from me—borrowed from my sister, Caroline—and a diary with gold-edged paper and a tiny gold key to lock it from her parents.

"Isn't that precious. Every teen girl needs a special place to keep her private secrets," Betty's mother said. She speaks like that all the time. Words gush out of her mouth.

Betty unlocked the diary with the key and the Worm suddenly leapt into my mouth and said, "I have a diary."

Let me make this crystal clear. The Worm said it—not me. Anyway, the room got real quiet and Mother looked at me queerly, but I helped myself to a second piece of cake to let everyone know there's nothing especially special about having a diary.

Later, as we walked home, Mother said, "They must have used every sugar and butter ration coupon they had for that cake." A sigh of relief hissed from between my lips, because I thought Mother was going to get mad at me. She didn't but she did say, "I didn't know you kept a diary, Roberta. I hope you write in it every day. It'll help your penmanship." And she looked at me very hard, so that was almost as bad as her being mad.

That is how it happens I'm writing in this old math notebook. *Wretched Worm!*

Thursday, September 16, 1943

I borrowed some of Caroline's red nail polish and wrote D-I-A-R-Y in big letters across my notebook. It looks pretty good, though some of the bristles from the brush got stuck in the polish and smeared when I fished them out. I put polish on my nails, too, since the bottle was open anyway. Hope Caroline doesn't notice.

Friday, September 17, 1943

Caroline noticed. She yelled at me and told Mother she needed her own room.

Mother said calmly, "You can sleep in the attic if you want."

I laughed because you have to bend over double to walk in our attic. Everyone shares a bedroom in our house: Mother and Dad downstairs, Caroline and me upstairs, and Brian and Stephen across the hall from us. Alex used to share with them until he went to war.

Caroline slammed our bedroom door, making the walls shake, and screamed at me, "Stay on your own side, you little creep."

She has a fearful temper. It makes her freckles stand out brilliant red, which matches quite nicely with her red hair. If Alex were here he'd say, "You won't miss a little bit of nail polish, Caroline." Alex always takes my side.

Caroline is eighteen and started working this past summer, after graduating high school, in the filing room at London Life Insurance downtown. She wears bright red lipstick. Grandma says Caroline is the beauty in our family and I know I'm not the brains (that's Alex), so I'm not sure what I am.

Caroline goes out to dances and stuff all the time. When Mother said to her, "You're doing too much running around", Caroline replied, "All work and no play makes Jill a dull girl."

Mother said, "Dull girl, indeed! She thinks she's the cat's meow these days, that girl." That is so true.

> *Dear Mother and Dad and all,*
> *I spent such a night as I wouldn't want to again.*
> *These flying bombs are around. For two hours I lay*
> *listening to their noise, and then suddenly they'd*
> *stop to be followed by a bang. All the windows of the*
> *house have been blasted but one.*

Saturday, September 18, 1943

I don't think I'll write in this book any more.

11

Friday, September 24, 1943

Tonight at supper Mother said, "Henry (that's Dad), Roberta is keeping a diary. She writes in it every day."

Dad looked at me and said, "Is that right, Bobby. That's a good girl."

I don't know why writing a diary makes me good. I just wish Mother hadn't said anything at supper in front of everyone. Especially Brian. You'd think at fifteen he'd grow up and stop teasing me. Guess I'm writing in my diary again. *Glum!*

Saturday, September 25, 1943

Went to the movies with Betty and Lydia and we saw *Only Angels Have Wings*, with Rita Hayworth and Cary Grant. Betty's *ambition* in life is to be an actress like Rita Hayworth. She practises walking like her all the time, though I have noticed that Rita sort of glides while Betty plods, but Lydia and I tell her she's a spitting image anyway.

Before the movie there was a newsreel of the war. It showed men riding on tanks and others marching in long lines behind. I studied each face carefully, hoping to see Alex. It's hard to tell the soldiers apart because they are all dressed the same and, even though I try to concentrate, I soon mix up one face with the next.

After the movie I went to visit Aunt Lily. She lives around the corner from us and was working in her garden when I got there. Aunt Lily is Mother's baby sister. She is beautiful even with her blonde hair tied up in a kerchief and dirt smeared on her cheek. You'd think she'd make everyone around her feel plain and ordinary, but she doesn't. For some reason being with Aunt Lily makes me feel beautiful, too. Betty's also very pretty, but being around her makes me feel awkward and clumsy.

Uncle Billy is Aunt Lily's husband and he's very handsome. Better even than Cary Grant. They'd only been married a year when Uncle Billy became a soldier. That's been pretty near three years now.

Aunt Lily's garden is her pride and joy. I love it, too, because it has a *profusion* of flowers and is peaceful. Our grass is trampled to mud by Brian's friends playing football, and Mother keeps a Victory vegetable garden instead of flowers. The government says it is patriotic to grow our own food so we don't take it from the mouths of our fighting soldiers overseas. Aunt Lily says she doesn't eat much so she keeps a regular garden. Right now there are still yellow mums and late pink roses blooming in Aunt Lily's garden.

"What are those flowers?" I asked, pointing at long ropes of brilliant red blooms hanging over the brown wooden fence at the back of the yard.

"That's called love-lies-bleeding," Aunt Lily replied. She stared at the red flowers a moment, then shivered all over and her face went white. "That's a gruesome name for a flower," she said. "Why on earth did I ever put those in?"

"I think it's a romantic name," I told her. I'll write and tell Alex that name because he loves words.

> *I received the photos. It was nice to have seen some*
> *of the flower garden back there for this is the first*
> *summer I have not been home and my first over here*
> *and wonder if another will come around.*

> *Sunday, September 26, 1943*

Sunday school and church this morning, then Mother said I had to write my letters to Alex and Uncle Billy.

"But I can never think of anything to say," I complained.

"Tell them about school, your friends," Mother said. "It's important and comforting to them to know life is normal here. Heaven knows, it's not normal there."

So I wrote Alex about the Worm of Jealousy and keeping a diary and how I was making a list of interesting words for him when he gets back.

One time Alex told me he'd like to be a writer for a newspaper. He told me words for him were like paint for an artist and they both made pictures. Dad said he'd speak to the foreman at the foundry where he works about a job when Alex finished school. I don't think Alex ever told Dad he wanted to be a newspaperman. It doesn't matter any way because he joined the army right after graduation.

Mother says, "It's all that school principal's fault putting such notions in those boys' heads. Telling them to join the forces or be labelled a coward. And you know Alex, he takes things so to heart. All that principal's fault."

I think it's the factory's fault, but Alex would have joined the army anyway because he's Alex.

September 27, 1943
Monday morning before school

We got a letter from Alex from over at the war. Mother held it tight to her chest with both hands and closed her eyes. Then she opened them, sighed, and set the letter against the salt shaker to read at supper when Dad was home. When she wasn't looking I took it and studied the envelope. On the back Alex had written his name and a bunch of numbers. There are three round circles stamped on it. One says *Field Post Office*, one says *Passed by Censor 9112*, and the last says *1st Canadian Corp*. I think of all the hands that have touched Alex's letter before mine.

Monday, September 27, 1943
After supper

Alex is in Sicily. Stephen put a red pin on the map of Europe he cut from the newspaper and taped to the wall near the radio. The head of the pin covered the entire island of Sicily. I try to picture Alex somewhere in Sicily writing this letter, holding a pencil in his hand (we're sending him a new pen for Christmas), chewing the end when he's thinking. I picture him writing while sitting in a chair in front of a wobbly, wooden table; then I picture him sitting on the edge of a narrow, hard bed; then sitting outside with his back against a crumbled brick wall, his knees drawn up to write on. I try the sun shining, then I try it raining. I picture bombs exploding near him, but then wish I hadn't because that is too scary. But no matter what I try, it doesn't work. I can't picture him writing this letter at all. I can't picture him anywhere but at our house and sometimes...I can't even picture Alex here any more.

Tuesday, September 28, 1943

I asked Dad why he doesn't wear a white shirt and tie to work every day like Betty's father does. He said, "A tie would get caught in the machinery and then where would I be?—my head chopped off, that's where. Ties and machinery don't go together. Bankers don't have to worry about that."

Mother thumped the iron hard on the board and glared at me. What did I do?

> *I've had enough of troopship life...it is so crowded*
> *one can hardly move and trying to get space to even*
> *sit is bad enough.*

Wednesday, September 29, 1943

I am so glad I have someone to walk to school with. I was waiting at the end of the street for Betty and Lydia to come by when I saw Nancy Goddard walking to school by herself. Walking to school by yourself is death.

Thursday, September 30, 1943
After school

Mrs. Ford, our Domestic Arts teacher, asked the Grade Eight girls to stay every Monday and Thursday after school to form a knitting club to knit winter socks and scarves for the soldiers. She says the younger girls are part of the Junior Red Cross and we older girls should do our bit to help the war effort. Betty says she'll ask her dad for money to buy socks because she isn't taking up knitting. Lydia says that's what she'll do, too. So I guess I'll ask Dad for money.

Thursday, September 30, 1943
Before bed

I told Mother and Dad about the knitting club. Brian laughed so hard he fell off the sofa. He said, "Obviously, Mrs. Ford has never seen your knitting." I gave him a *withering* glance.

I told Dad that Betty's and Lydia's fathers were going to donate money to buy socks so they didn't have to knit and could I have some money, too. Mother whacked me across the back of my head and sent me directly to bed. She is so unfair.

Friday, October 1, 1943

At supper Brian asked me if the Worm of Jealousy was still in my stomach and, if so, perhaps I should see the doctor. I was so mad my legs shook and I thought I was having a heart attack because I couldn't breathe. I jumped out of my chair and screamed, "You bastard!" I'd never actually said that word out loud before, though I'd often thought it in connection with Brian. Mother sent us both directly to bed, which I thought very unfair. I was the one wronged here. I told Mother Brian read my diary.

She said, "Young ladies do not swear, no matter how angry they are."

I said, "Well, he is a bastard (twice in one day) and he's been reading my diary."

I'm just sorry Aunt Lily was here to witness my shame, and it must have upset her terribly because her face was beet red and her shoulders shook in distress. Stephen kept eating through it all! At least I didn't have to do the dishes.

Saturday, October 2, 1943

Dad says Brian has to make me a wooden box with a lock and key to keep my diary in as an apology. When Dad left the room I told Brian, "I wish you were at the war instead of Alex."

Brian said, "Well, two and a half more years and I will be and I won't have to see your ugly face any more." I know he just said that because he's mad. I'm not really ugly, am I?

> *I have been kicking myself to get a letter off to you as soon as possible as you may have forgotten all about me…*

Sunday, October 3, 1943

Betty wanted me to visit her today, but Mother said Sunday is for family spending time together, not gallivanting around town. I told her Nancy Goddard gallivants on Sundays and she's the minister's daughter.

Mother said, "If Nancy Goddard jumped off a bridge would you do it, too?"

What that has to do with visiting Betty I'm sure I don't know. I went to Aunt Lily's instead, because she's family, and had tea in her garden.

"We'll enjoy the last of the warm weather," Aunt Lily said, carrying out a tray with cups and cookies. Aunt Lily is the only one who understands that I'm an adult now and can drink tea.

"Do you have a cold starting?" I asked, because Aunt Lily's eyes were red and there was a big crease across her forehead.

"The house is a little big for me today, Bobby," she told me. "I'm thinking of renting it out and moving in with Mother until Billy comes home."

By Mother she means Grandma. Aunt Lily wouldn't be very happy living with Grandma. She and Aunt Lily don't see eye to eye on things, Mother said. Mostly on Uncle Billy. Grandma thought Uncle Billy a layabout because he couldn't find a job, and she didn't want Aunt Lily to marry him, but Aunt Lily told her, "Times are hard and jobs are scarce. Lots of men are out of work. Billy's a good man and I'm marrying him."

Grandma shouldn't be mad now because Uncle Billy has a job in the army.

I don't want Aunt Lily to move for a purely selfish reason. I love her garden.

"The house seems the same size as usual to me," I assured her and she laughed and the crease smoothed out of her forehead.

Monday, October 4, 1943

Mrs. Ford says if the soldiers fought like I knitted, the war would have been over long ago—and we would have lost. Nancy says she'll help me with my knitting if I like.

Tuesday, October 5, 1943

Betty said, "If you want to take knitting lessons from Nancy it is completely up to you but, really, Nancy Goddard isn't our sort."

I guess I'll tell Nancy tomorrow my mother is going to teach me instead. I know that's a lie, but is it still a lie if the lie is told so someone's feelings aren't hurt? I would think in this case the fact I'm trying not to hurt Nancy would cancel out the lie. I wonder what sort Betty and I are?

Wednesday, October 6, 1943
Afternoon, immediately after school

Rick Anderson spoke to me today! He sits in front of me in Science and is so handsome. Even the back of his head is so good-looking I miss what the teacher says sometimes because I'm admiring it. He turned around in his desk before class and said, "Hey, can I borrow your homework? I didn't have time to finish mine."

I said, "Sure," except it came out like a gulpy fish gasp.

Afterward, I thought I should have said something clever like, "Hope you can read my writing" or "Why should I give you my homework?" and pouted. Betty would have done that. Still, he talked to ME and I talked to HIM. I'll practise clever things to say when I'm in bed tonight so I'll be ready for tomorrow. Nancy said it was very nice my mother was going to teach me knitting.

Two days ago there were prayer services all over this country. I guess you people had one too. Anyhow we fellows in the army went to a service. Whether it does any good I don't know.

19

Thursday, October 7, 1943

I wrote down all the clever things I'd say on the front cover of my notebook so I could see it, but Rick Anderson never once turned in his seat. He threw paper airplanes across the room instead. *Forlorn!*

A letter came today from Alex from over at the war. Mother says she doesn't like what she's reading between the lines. She says Alex sounds lonely. I took the letter after she'd read it and studied it, but I couldn't see anything between the lines except empty space. Mother must be mistaken. Alex says it's very hot in Sicily and they eat a lot of oranges and nuts. We've had some very nice sunny days here, but the nights are beginning to get cold. On the way home from Aunt Lily's last night I got goose bumps on my legs the size of chicken eggs. I didn't tell Mother because she'd make me wear thick stockings. Wearing thick stockings to school is death. Only the little kids wear them. Alex asked us to send him more cigarettes. I can't believe he smokes so many!

Friday, October 8, 1943

Betty says I must have my period by now because I'm thirteen. I hate when Betty and Lydia talk about periods and stuff. It makes my head spin and my stomach hurt. When I got home I took out the secret book Mother gave me and read it again, just in case I'd had my period and didn't know it. The book says I'd notice a bit of spotting on my underpants and that would be my period.

Friday October 8, 1943
Late

Before bed, Dad turned on the radio to hear Lorne Greene on CBC news like every night and Mother said, "Turn that off. I don't want to hear war news any more." So Dad went to turn it off but Mother suddenly yelled, "No, leave it on."

"Well make up your mind," Dad said. "Stop dithering."

Mother threw her apron at him and said, "I've never dithered in my life." And she started to cry. Dad turned off the radio and rubbed her shoulder.

Saturday, October 9, 1943

Mother cleared the table in the kitchen and told me and Caroline we had to stay in today, because she was doing a large baking and needed help. Betty was real mad when I telephoned her and said I couldn't go to the movies. She said, "Best friends go to the movies together."

I tried desperately hard to assure her I'd go except Mother said no. I know she and Lydia will go together without me and Lydia will be Betty's best friend today.

Mother said she hoped nobody minded that she was using all the sugar and butter ration coupons. We each of us have our own ration coupon book from the government for meat and other food that is in short supply, but Mother keeps them all. She says she needs a suitcase to carry them about to the stores, as having so many makes her purse bulge. She'd been saving from our rations for the last couple of weeks so she could bake for Alex's' and Uncle Billy's Christmas Packages. We'd be short for the next while, but they would have nice parcels to open. I cut up red and green cherries for hours. My fingers are still sticky and bright red on the ends.

> *I hope you all have a very good Christmas this year.*
> *I sure would like to be there and have the day at*
> *home. These days my mind goes back to the good old*
> *days and the Xmas's we used to have.*

Sunday, October 10, 1943

It's the day before Thanksgiving. Reverend Goddard said we should be thankful for what we have in these hard times, and I am, it's just I want what Betty has too, and then I know I'd be twice as thankful.

Starting right after church we packed the Christmas Package for Alex. Last year Alex didn't get the Package until July! We put in razor blades, Laura Secord chocolates (I wanted one of them so bad. I haven't had chocolate in so long.), socks (not knitted by me), Christmas cookies, fruit cake, *Reader's Digest* magazines, cheese, biscuits, Ivory soap, chocolate powdered drink, handkerchiefs and a wool sweater. I put in my present, a book about Canadian birds. Alex likes identifying all the different birds, and even though it's about Canadian birds, I'm sending it anyway. Maybe some of our birds are over at the war, too. Mother and Dad bought Alex a new watch. Caroline gave him a new fountain pen and writing paper, and Brian gave him a Johnny Canuck comic book.

The front of the comic book showed Johnny Canuck rescuing a beautiful girl from the clutches of a German soldier. I told Brian it was stupid looking, but actually I'd love to be rescued in the nick of time by Rick Anderson. Stephen gave Alex a drawing of a plane he'd made. Then Brian, as usual, caused a big ruckus. He said, "When you do my Christmas parcel when I go to war, I don't want any soap, just an extra box of chocolates."

Mother whirled so fast, the palm of her hand hit the back of Brian's head with a *smack* we all heard. "You stop that kind of talk!" Mother yelled. "You're not going to war. You think it's all a game. Well, people die in war. Young people just like you. They're the ones who die, the young people."

Brian's mouth opened and shut like a dying fish and it should have been funny, except it wasn't.

After a while Dad said, "Doesn't seem to be much room left in that box. I'll send the cigarettes separate."

Monday, October 11, 1943

No school today because it's Thanksgiving. Aunt Lily picked up Grandma in her car to bring her for supper. Dad said, "That's a terrible waste of gas ration."

Mother glared at him fiercely.

At the dinner table Grandma said to me, "I hope you appreciate the fact you're having turkey today when lots of people overseas have nothing."

So I tried hard to appreciate the turkey. I tried to imagine having no food and being hungry, but I couldn't because I've never been hungry and the gravy was too *tantalizing* to resist. Brian ate two helpings of everything: mashed potatoes, turkey, carrots and pumpkin pie, like the pig he is. I wonder if Alex had Thanksgiving.

Tuesday, October 12, 1943

Back to school. Nothing new to report on the Rick Anderson front. In Domestic Arts today we made pancakes. It's the first time Mrs. Ford let us near the stove. Betty, Lydia and I were in a group, but Mrs. Ford said there had to be a fourth so she told Nancy Goddard to join us. Our pancakes were kind of flat, but with lots of syrup you barely noticed the burned parts.

Betty said, "It doesn't matter to me if I learn to cook because after I get married I'll have servants do that for me."

Nancy said it was a cruel sort of punishment to make us eat our own *concoctions*. (Nancy's word but I liked it so much I borrowed it for my list.)

Stephen came to my room while I was writing in my diary. He

asked, "Do you think the war will end soon?"

"I don't know," I answered.

"I just wondered is all," he said.

I noticed then how white he was. "Why do you care?" I asked him.

"I don't want to be a soldier," he said. I could tell he was near crying. "I'd be scared all the time."

"Kids don't become soldiers," I told him. "You're just scared now because you're a kid. If you were grown up, you wouldn't be scared at all."

"Do you think so?" he asked.

"Yep," I said. I pulled him into my bed and put the quilt over both our heads, because I didn't really believe myself.

I've had a few close calls and believe me I dig in and never ever felt like digging a hole as I do some days here and in record time too.

Wednesday, October 13, 1943

Nancy Goddard went in through the BOYS' door at school today. She said it was no different from going through our door except the principal, Mr. Smith, was waiting on the other side and gave her a detention. Betty says it was scandalous and Nancy should go in the BOYS' door every day, because she acts more like a boy than a girl.

Thursday, October 14, 1943

I watched Stephen on the boys' side of the playground at recess. He was playing by himself with one of his fighter planes. You could almost forget Stephen is around, he's so quiet and well-behaved. Mother says he's the easiest of us all to raise. Stephen loves his airplanes and can tell you the names of every one of them. Brian told him once that his planes were made of metal and the government wanted everyone's metal to melt down and make real planes for the war effort, and Stephen would have to give them his toy plane. Stephen looked at his plane for a moment, then held it out to Brian to give to the government. Brian slapped Stephen's hand away and got real mad for nothing. "Can't you tell when someone's pulling your leg!" he yelled.

Stephen is the baby of our family, but at times he seems the oldest.

Friday, October 15, 1943

Ours is the most popular house on the street today. Kids ride miles on their bicycles to gather chestnuts from our tree, because our tree has the biggest, brownest chestnuts in the world. Mrs. Turner next door gets mad at the kids leaving their bicycles on the sidewalk while they collect chestnuts, making it so "decent people can't even walk around." Sometimes there's twenty bikes or more.

One year Brian thought he'd make people pay a penny for every five chestnuts they took. We collected a lot of money until Mother found out. She made him give the money back. "What if God made you pay each time you looked at his beautiful tree?" she asked.

I still thought it a very *enterprising* idea of Brian's.

With a nail, we hammer holes through the chestnuts and thread white string through them and play "conkers" until the sidewalk is littered with broken chestnuts. I hoard my keeper though. Every year I pick the shiniest chestnut and polish it until it gleams like Mother's mahogany dining room table. I have a whole collection now. I don't tell Betty about it because she'd think I was childish.

Saturday, October 16, 1943
Morning

Mother came into the bedroom and handed me a package. "It's a training bra," she said. "Do you know how to put it on?"

I told her "yes" and felt my face heating up red. I feel two ways about this bra. I've been wanting one because Betty and Lydia wear one and I don't want to be left out. I don't want one because the boys (and some of the girls too) pull the elastic out the back and snap it on your bare skin, and everyone in class knows what that *snap* means. Helen Taylor cried when her bra was snapped in class. I can't figure out though why they call it a training bra. What am I training for?

Saturday, October 16, 1943
After supper

I'm pretending to write in my diary, but really I'm watching Caroline to see how she wears her bra. She is sitting at her dressing table in her housecoat putting on rouge and powder. She is going to the club where the girls dance and play cards with visiting service men. She's a hostess. I spent the morning in the bathroom trying on my training bra. At first it nearly strangled me under my chin so I adjusted the straps. Those tiny clips are so stupid, they hurt your fingers. Then I realized that you could see the bra through my blouse and I thought that looked awful, so I put on my undershirt over the bra to go to the movies with Betty and Lydia. We saw *The Count of Monte Cristo*, but my new bra was very uncomfortable so I don't remember much of the movie.

Caroline has brushed her hair into a roll and is spraying it all over. Funny, I never noticed before how Caroline wears her bra, though I must have watched her dress a million times. Now she's doing her lipstick, leaning forward close to the mirror and dabbing some on the top part of her lip where it goes up into two peaks.

"What are you looking at?" She caught me staring.

"Nothing. Just thinking," I said. I creased my forehead and bit my lip to look thoughtful.

Finally, she stood and dropped her housecoat to the floor and put on her blouse, *without an undershirt,* so I guess it's okay to see a bra through the blouse.

Next she turned her perfume bottle upside down on her finger, then touched the scented finger behind her ears and on her wrists. Saturday night sure takes a lot of work. Finally, she turned and stretched to see every part of herself in the dresser mirror.

"We need a full-length mirror," she complained. "These are awful stockings, so thick. I'll be glad when the war's over and we can get some decent silk hose." Then, "Well, ta-ta, dear," she said and waggled her fingers at me. Caroline seems very happy these days.

> *Do you remember the Allens who used to live on*
> *Yonge Street? Well, his boy is in Signals and I met*
> *him on the boat. He says does not know where his*
> *mother and father are and they never write.*

Sunday, October 17, 1943

I'm never going downstairs in this house again. Even if I starve to death. Here is why: Caroline came in very late last night and was still sleeping when I left for Sunday school. She wasn't with Mother and Dad at church, either. Dad's face looked like a thundercloud and I thought, Caroline's going to get it.

But when we got home from church, Caroline had made sandwiches and set out lettuce and green onions (Dad's favourite) for lunch. She had on her bright red lipstick, even though she didn't go to church. After lunch Caroline turned on the radio and found some dance music. She grabbed Dad by the hands and hauled him out of his chair.

"No. No," Dad protested. "I've just eaten."

But Caroline dragged him into the middle of the room and soon he was dancing and twirling her around. I wanted to dance with Dad, too, so I ran upstairs and put on some of Caroline's red lipstick. I ran back down and grabbed Dad's hands, but he looked at my red lips and yelled, "You go right back up those stairs, Missy, and take that stuff off your face. No daughter of mine is going around all tarted up."

"But Caroline—" I started to say.

But Dad yelled, "No back talk!"

Caroline is definitely Dad's favourite. Well, I know I'm Alex's favourite, but he's not here. I'm never going downstairs again.

Sunday, October 17, 1943
Before bed

I went downstairs and listened to Jack Benny, the comedian, on the radio, but I didn't speak to Dad. He's very funny. (Jack Benny, not Dad.)

Monday, October 18, 1943

I felt so wretched inside I put a foot over into the boys' yard. At least I think it was the boys' yard. There is not an actual line to separate us. Everyone just knows which is the girls' side and which is the boys' side.

I said to Betty, "It's just plain stupid we can't be outside together, when we're inside together all the time."

She looked at me like I'd lost my mind. "Girls are always separated from the boys," she said. "Besides, they play rough."

Recess is stupid, too. All we do is stand around and talk at the fence at the back of the yard. And the boys stand at the fence on their side and punch each other and talk. Occasionally they play catch.

I thought it very brave of me to put my foot over on the boys' side, because I could have got the strap. You get the strap whether you're a girl or a boy. They don't separate that.

I'm still wearing an undershirt over my bra.

It is very hard to say what the outlook and promises
of peace will be right now, that has us all guessing.

Tuesday, October 19, 1943

Brian has joined the cadets at school. "Practising for the real thing," he announced at supper. I waited for Mother to explode but she just looked sad.

Wednesday, October 20, 1943

At recess Betty squealed loudly and snapped my bra from beneath my undershirt. Rick Anderson looked over at the commotion. I could have just smacked her.

A letter came from Alex over at the war. Stephen asked Dad what exactly Alex was doing over at the war. Dad says, "No one knows what they're doing over there. But if you mean his job, he's in the infantry." It took four weeks for this letter to come over from the war.

Thursday, October 21, 1943

Mrs. Ford took the socks I was knitting and unravelled them. Then she gave me the wool and thicker needles and said to try knitting a scarf. Nancy said, "Mrs. Ford's just a little crabby these days because she's expecting."

"Expecting what?" I asked after I waited for Nancy to finish her sentence and she didn't.

"A baby, of course," Nancy whispered. "Can you see her and Mr. Ford making a baby?" She *grimaced.*

Mr. Ford is a butcher and has two chins that wobble like a turkey's wattle when he speaks. His face is shiny and he always has a bead of perspiration (though Nancy says it's snot because she's so rude) on the end of his nose. I try to imagine Mrs. Ford and Mr. Ford making a baby, but I can't because I haven't the slightest idea how a baby is made. I didn't want Nancy to know that I don't know so I gave her a wise, knowing smile. Mrs. Ford asked me if I felt all right because my face was all screwed up like I was in pain.

> *I am unable to tell you about where I am as yet for*
> *many reasons. Some day soon will be able to tell you*
> *many interesting things of places and people.*

Friday, October 22, 1943

Another letter came from Alex over at the war. He said that he felt fine and asked for cigarettes. Brian thought it was a dumb letter and wondered why he never writes about the fighting.

"He can't tell us very much," Dad told him. "Letters from overseas are censored so the enemy doesn't know our battle plans. Wouldn't want those letters to fall into the wrong hands."

"In cadets," Brian said, "they told us there might be spies anywhere. Your next-door neighbour could be a spy."

I thought about Mrs. Turner complaining about the bicycles on the sidewalk. I don't see her as a spy.

"You have to watch everything you say," he told us. "One lady's husband, a soldier, phoned her from England and said they were shipping out to France and told her the date and boat they were leaving on, and she told her father, who told a man at his office, who was really a spy, not an office worker, and the Germans torpedoed the boat. You can't trust anyone."

We all looked around at each other and the room was very quiet. Stephen's eyes were huge. Suddenly the door slammed and we all jumped. Even Dad and Brian. It was just Caroline home from work.

Saturday, October 23, 1943

Went to the movies with Betty and Lydia. The newsreel showed soldiers in Sicily and I wanted to tell Betty and Lydia that's where Alex was, but I remembered that there might be spies sitting next to us, so I kept quiet. I raced all the way home to tell Mother and she went to the movie that very night just to see where Alex was. I babysat the little brats two doors down. They sure made me work, but I was running out of money for the movies.

I have to find out how babies are made. I feel like everyone in the world knows this but me.

Sunday, October 24, 1943

After church today I was reading the Saturday comics—I like Wash Tubb and Henry—and I turned the page and there was the Honour Roll—all the people wounded, missing or killed over at the war. I didn't want to read it, but I couldn't not read it. I thought about how awful it would be if one day I saw Alex's name there, then immediately felt horrified in case thinking it made it come true. I quickly turned to the Dorothy Dix advice column on the women's page, but it didn't help even though it was about *philandering* husbands. All day I felt like a huge, black cloud was hanging over me.

CANADIAN PACIFIC TELEGRAPHS

ALL WELL AND SAFE WRITE SAME ADDRESS

Monday, October 25, 1943

I was coming home from school for lunch when the telegram boy whizzed past on his bike. When I turned into our street I saw his bike leaning against the chestnut tree in front of our house. My heart began to pound and my stomach hurt something awful. I remembered the Honour Roll and the dark feeling rushed back. I reminded myself that the really bad telegrams come after supper, but my mind wouldn't believe me. I began running and caught up to Aunt Lily, who'd seen the boy pass also.

"Everything's fine," Mother assured us when we ran up out of breath. "Billy and Alex sent a telegram to say they are together in Italy and they're safe."

"That does it," Aunt Lily said. "I'm getting a job tomorrow."

Tuesday, October 26, 1943

A beautiful day—the air is so warm, I'm sitting in the backyard writing in my diary. The sun is like liquid gold washing over me. The last of the leaves are floating down gently, red and yellow. Everything would be perfect—except Brian and his friends are making so much noise playing football.

Just like she said, Aunt Lily went out and got a job at Central Aircraft Limited fixing airplane engines. I heard Mother speaking to Dad last night.

"She needs something to keep her busy or she'll go crazy. And I know how she feels. Sometimes I think a job would do me good, too, but at least I have all of you to take care of and my Red Cross volunteer work. Lily has no one."

Wednesday, October 27, 1943

Last night we had a bad storm and the wind blew the rest of the chestnuts down. I lay in bed listening to them bounce off the roof. Today it turned cold and rained.

> *It rains very hard at times and how, it just pours down...*

Thursday, October 28, 1943

I borrowed some of Caroline's perfume hoping to *entice* Rick Anderson. I sat in class with my clever sayings ready in front of me, but all Rick said was "What stinks?"

At knitting club, Mrs. Ford asked if my scarf would be ready for this war or the next one. I tried to stop it but a big tear dropped out of my eye onto my wool. I was utterly *humiliated.*

Nancy said, "Never mind. If we had to live with Mr. Ford's chins day in and day out, we'd be awfully grumpy too."

I don't know if Betty would like the fact that Nancy talks to me.

Friday, October 29, 1943

A horrible day! Betty and Lydia weren't at the corner so I had to walk to school alone. Then they weren't at school either. At lunch I telephoned Betty, but there was no answer at her house so I had to walk back to school alone too. I'm sure everyone was watching me and thinking how awful a person I must be that no one wanted to walk with me. I tried to pretend it didn't matter to me, but it did. I just started crying again thinking about it. My life is horrible.

Saturday, October 30, 1943

I must be getting sick. I can't explain why I keep crying. I have a *perpetually* red nose. Brian asked why my eyes were leaking so much lately. I waited all day for Betty to call to go to the movies, but she didn't. I helped Stephen get his Hallowe'en costume ready. He wanted to be a pilot, so I borrowed Brian's cadet uniform and Dad's welding glasses and tied mother's good silk scarf around his neck. Hallowe'en was tonight because the real night was Sunday and you can't have Hallowe'en on Sunday.

> *It seems a long time…5 weeks, to not have a letter*
> *from anyone.*

Sunday, October 31, 1943

Sunday school, church and boring letters. I could just die from all the excitement. I almost told Mother about Caroline coming in at two o'clock in the morning, but today at church Rev. Goddard said to "erase the pettiness from our hearts and minds" so I didn't tell on her and felt very righteous all day, though that was wearing off by supper. I wonder if missionaries feel righteous all the time or if once in a while they feel like being petty just for a change.

Aunt Lily came to supper and didn't once stop talking about her job overhauling engines at the aircraft plant. I was bored to the limit of my *endurance.*

Monday, November 1, 1943

I found out that Betty's mother had taken Betty and Lydia by train to Toronto for a shopping trip. Betty said she could only pick one friend to go and Lydia's name came before mine in the alphabet so she thought that was a fair way to pick.

I pointed out to her that *B* comes before *L*, but she said, "No, silly, your real name begins with an *R*. Roberta."

I guess she's right. Except I can't help but think if she'd really wanted me to go, my name would have begun with a *B*.

Had a letter from Alex over at the war. It seems he and Uncle Billy are in the same unit, which has Mother and Aunt Lily very excited. "I'm glad Billy is there to keep an eye on Alex," Mother said happily.

"And vice versa," Aunt Lily said. Except her mouth wasn't smiling. "I've heard stories down at the plant about what some of the men get up to over there."

"Lily!" Mother whispered. She rolled her eyes meaningfully at me.

"Sorry," Aunt Lily said, looking quite *contrite*. "All the overtime at work is putting me out of sorts, and I haven't seen Billy for so long I almost forget what he looks like."

Tuesday, November 2, 1943

After supper I asked Mother if she'd take me and Betty on a shopping trip to Toronto on Friday. She looked quite amazed and repeated, "A shopping trip! What on earth put that idea into your head. Besides, that's a school day and you aren't missing school to go shopping. Of all the ideas!"

I felt my eyes threatening to leak so I ran upstairs. Caroline came up later and gave me a skirt that didn't fit her any more, and said she'd help me to shorten it. It's very pretty with red and green checks.

Wednesday, November 3, 1943

We had our first snow overnight, though it disappeared by lunchtime. Mother insisted I wear stockings to school and I thought I'd die of embarrassment, but when I got to school I saw several other girls wearing them, too. Betty and Lydia still wore socks. "The Betsy Twins," Nancy calls them. We had a mathematics test today that I completely forgot about so I wasn't prepared.

Thursday, November 4, 1943

Mother said she would take me on Saturday for shopping and lunch if I wanted, though she had no money to buy anything. I said, "In Toronto?" and she said, "No, London is perfectly fine. You can ask a friend if you want. Why don't you ask Nancy Goddard. She seems like a nice girl."

"I want to ask Betty," I told her.

"Suit yourself," Mother said.

Betty accepted my invitation "with delight." She has *impeccable* manners. I cannot say the same for Nancy.

I didn't do very well on my mathematics test so I hid it in my underwear drawer until after Saturday to show Mother.

Friday, November 5, 1943

I am very excited about our shopping trip—so excited I almost forgot about Rick Anderson, until I saw him at school. He is so handsome. We had to fill out a form at school that asked us how tall we were, how much we weighed and the colour of our hair. Nancy wrote her hair colour as "dog-poop brown." Betty said Nancy was totally disgusting. Thinking about it, my hair is dog-poop brown, too.

Bully beef and hardtack, that was our chief food both in Sicily and Italy.

Saturday, November 6, 1943

Betty's father was going to work, so he dropped Betty off early in the morning. I rushed her right past the kitchen where Stephen, Brian and Dad were having breakfast and up the stairs to my bedroom. I was *mortified* that Caroline was still in bed, but she looks very pretty even when she sleeps. Betty was amazed at all the makeup Caroline has. I let Betty try some of Caroline's perfume. There was only one sticky moment. On the way out, Dad and Brian came out of the kitchen and Mother said, "Bobby, introduce your friend to your father and brother."

"They're in their undershirts," I said, *mortified* for the second time that morning.

"They're clean undershirts, dear. I know, I washed them myself," Mother said. I could tell by her voice she was getting mad, so I quickly muttered an introduction. Betty was very gracious to Dad and dimpled at Brian, though she must have been as *mortified* as me. I've never seen Betty's dad in anything except a shirt and tie, even on a Saturday morning. He probably even sleeps in a shirt and tie.

We took the bus downtown. We went to Kingsmills department store. Their front window had a huge picture of the king and queen and flags and photographs of soldiers. One sign said, "The measure of a man has always been his readiness to fight in a just cause." It almost made me wish I was a man so I could be a soldier.

Betty showed us her mother's dish pattern in the china department. The plates were so thin I could see my hand through them. Mother declared the dishes were "absolutely lovely, but wouldn't last two minutes in our house."

We had lunch in a tea room downtown. I had a tuna salad sandwich and Betty had chicken salad. I immediately realized I should have ordered chicken salad as it was much more elegant-sounding than tuna.

While we ate, Betty told us all about the luncheon she'd had in Toronto and the sweet little cups of lemon-scented water given to them to wash their fingers in after they ate. She said that our lunch compared "very favourably." Sometimes when Betty speaks that way it sounds just like her mother talking.

Betty showed us the shoes at Rowland Hill's shoe store she is going to ask her father for. They were grand. Mother said they were quite dear, though I think she was referring to their price, not their looks.

Betty asked me a lot of questions about Brian on the bus ride home and seemed quite impressed when I said he was a cadet. That was probably the only time in my life I've bragged about Brian.

It was an absolutely perfect day.

Sunday, November 7, 1943

Sunday school and church and letters. It's raining and extremely windy today. Aunt Lily came to supper. She said, "The job helps, but I'm still very lonely. I think I might take in a boarder. There's lots of girls down at the plant looking for a place to stay. They have them all doubled up at the YWCA as so many have come to London to work. in the factories now that most men are gone overseas."

I said, "If you're lonely, why don't you have a baby? I mean, you're married now."

Dad dropped his knife on his plate and it made a terrible clatter. It's a good thing it wasn't as thin as Betty's mother's plates.

After the dishes were done and Aunt Lily thought I'd gone upstairs, I heard her speaking to Mother. "Haven't you told that girl anything yet?" she asked. "She's thirteen."

"I gave her a book. It tells her everything she needs to know right now," Mother said.

"She's growing up," Aunt Lily told Mother. "I'll tell her if you're too embarrassed."

"You'll do no such thing. Bobby is a very young girl still," Mother hissed.

"When did you tell Caroline?" Aunt Lily asked. There was a long silence, then Aunt Lily said, "You never told Caroline, did you? You're as bad as Mother. You'd better tell her before something happens."

"Oh, be quiet," Mother said irritably. And she sounded just like Caroline yelling at me.

It didn't take long once leaving England to get up
here near the front line right where the guns bark.
Over here you see more traffic than you ever did on
Yonge Street on a Sunday.

Monday, November 8, 1943

School again. I wish the older girls did something besides stand around and talk. I shiver the whole recess. At least skipping would keep me warm, but that's too babyish. I wore my new red and green checked skirt, and everyone told me how nice it looked. Betty said you'd never know it'd been Caroline's first. I told her it was very patriotic to wear remade clothes. She wanted to know how Brian was. I told her he was fine, but can't imagine why she'd care.

At knitting club after school Mrs. Ford said, "Knit, purl, knit, purl. That's all you have to remember, Bobby. Is knitting really that hard?"

Nancy has done two pairs of socks and is working on mittens. I wish I could quit the knitting club, except I think Mother would be very mad if I did.

I felt so bad I went to Aunt Lily's place and wandered around her garden. That didn't help to make me feel any better because it looks very sad. All the petals on the mums were browned at the edges, and the love-lies-bleeding had been ripped off the fence by the wind and lay wilted in red clumps on the dirt. For some reason, looking at them made me think of the Honour Roll in the newspaper.

Tuesday, November 9, 1943

I finally showed Mother my mathematics test. She wasn't very happy with my mark. She also wanted to know why I hadn't shown it to her sooner, because it was dated last Thursday. I told her I'd forgotten.

"What's it matter if a girl does math?" Brian said.

"Who do you think figures out the budget around here?" Mother told him. "Who does the shopping and takes care of the ration coupons and makes sure the bills are paid on time? If I'd failed mathematics I wouldn't do a very good job now, would I? It's important even for girls to know math."

Secretly, I agree with Brian. Why do I have to do math?

Wednesday, November 10, 1943

I woke up this morning and there was a huge red bump in the middle of my forehead—my first pimple! I tried to push it back in but that didn't help, it just hurt. At breakfast Brian said, "Hey, where'd that third eye come from?"

I told Mother I wasn't going to school.

"Don't be so silly. You are going to school," she said. "All teenagers have pimples. Besides, pride goeth before a fall."

I never know what she is talking about half the time.

I kept my head ducked down most of the day at school, except in history when Mr. Smith asked how could I see the blackboard with my face glued to my desk. I'm sure everyone saw my pimple.

There is a board over here and on it we can write
our guess when the war will end and sign our name.
I say if not the first of the year, it will be early
spring.

Thursday, November 11, 1943

It is Armistice Day and there is no school. Thank goodness. I look terrible. My pimple is *huge*!

Friday November 12, 1943

Spotting! The secret book said when I got my period I'd know because there'd be spotting. It said that crystal clear. That was an outright lie. Here is what really happened:

Mother was out packing clothes for bombed people in Britain when I got home from school. My head was aching. Then my stomach started hurting so much I could hardly walk. I went into the bathroom and there was blood all over my panties. I was too scared to leave the toilet. I thought something awful was wrong with me. I sat there crying, waiting for Mother to come home. Brian pounded on the door, but I yelled at him to go away, but he kept pounding on the door so I began screaming and then Mother arrived.

"What on earth is going on here?" she asked.

"Bobby won't let us in the bathroom," Brian said.

"Brian, stop that racket, and Bobby, open that door," Mother ordered.

I unlocked the door and hopped back on the toilet.

"I'm dying, Mother," I whispered. "Something's very wrong. I'm bleeding."

"You started your period, you silly ninny," Mother said. "That's all."

She gave me a sanitary napkin and a belt to wear around my waist to hold it in place. It's awfully uncomfortable.

Caroline just came into our bedroom, clucked her tongue and said, "Got the curse, huh?"

"The curse?" I asked

"Your period."

"The book said there'd only be spotting," I told her.

"Yeah, well, a man probably wrote the book," she said. "Look at it this way—you're growing up. Great, huh?"

Mother said the same thing when I got my pimple. What I'd like to know is what's so great about growing up. Just seems painful and yucky to me.

Saturday, November 13, 1943

All day I wondered if people knew I had my period. The napkin felt like a two-by-four! I know I waddle when I walk. I hate this. I wish I was born a boy. I didn't even go to the movies with Betty and Lydia.

This may be Sunday but it seems like any other day,
no rest for the wicked I suppose.

Sunday, November 14, 1943

At Sunday school Nancy Goddard asked me if I'd like to work with her in the nursery taking care of the babies while their parents were in church. "Sure. Anything's better than listening to Rev.

Goddard's sermons," I said, then remembered he was Nancy's father.

"Why do you think I'm down here?" she said.

Thank goodness she didn't seem offended.

Nancy was actually very *capable* with the babies. She knew how to diaper them and everything, but then she does have five younger brothers and sisters. "I'm going to have six babies when I grow up," she said.

"After you're married," I added.

"Preferably," she said, and laughed.

I hate this feeling of not knowing what everyone else knows.

After supper Dad was reading the paper and told us it said the war was going quite well and that we're winning.

"What I'd like to know," he said, "is if everything is going as well as the paper constantly tells us, why isn't it over?"

Monday, November 15, 1943

It was very cold today. Every time I spoke my breath hung in white puffs, and I pushed my face forward into the breath cloud. Finally, Betty asked, "What on earth are you doing?"

"Trying to see what my breath feels like," I said.

"When are you going to stop being such a child?" she sighed.

I almost told her about my period, but stopped myself when I remembered she'd snapped my bra strap.

Nancy was listening and said, "What if your words got trapped inside the puff and then you could hear them twice?"

I know exactly what she means.

Tuesday, November 16, 1943

Betty brought her dad's newspaper to school and we all read the Dorothy Dix column at recess. The boys wanted to know what we were giggling about, but Betty turned her back, pouted, and told them, "It's none of your beeswax." But I noticed she gave Rick Anderson a big smile, which made my heart sink.

It was all about middle-aged men flirting with girls young enough to be their daughters. Dorothy Dix says men like that are morons. She also says a girl cannot ask a boy out but has to wait until the boy asks the girl. Too bad, because I would ask out Rick Anderson. Or maybe not. He might say no, and then I'd be extremely embarrassed.

Wednesday, November 17, 1943

I asked Dad if he was middle-aged and he said, "Well, now that I think about it, I guess I am. Must have snuck up on me when I wasn't looking. Why do you ask?"

"No reason," I said. Perhaps I shouldn't have reminded him. Mother isn't very young any more, and I would hate Dad to be a moron. Maybe I should erase that last sentence.

> *I see where Freddi C— is listed among the missing*
> *in air operations over Berlin. It is too bad and very*
> *sorry to hear such news. That leaves only 2 boys in a*
> *family of 3 boys and 1 girl.*

Thursday, November 18, 1943

When I got home from school, there was a note from Mother telling me to put the potatoes and carrots she'd peeled on to cook. "Watch them CAREFULLY," the note said, as she'd be late coming home. Mother not being home after school always leaves me with a butterfly feeling in my stomach that something isn't quite right. She came in just before Dad got home from work but wouldn't say where

44

she'd been until we had eaten supper. Then she told us that Rev. Goddard's oldest boy, Brent, was missing, and she'd been to see Mrs. Goddard. I didn't know Nancy had a brother over at the war. There are so many Goddard children (at least eight) that I can't keep track of them.

Brian has moved the red pin into Italy where Alex is. He just guessed the place from reading the newspaper reports, because Alex hasn't told us exactly where he is. At least he isn't missing.

Just before bed, Mother told me that Mrs. Goddard had asked if I wanted to help at the Women's Auxiliary Dance on Saturday night because they were short-handed. They needed someone to take money at the door and someone to take coats. Nancy was helping out and I'd been invited to stay overnight with her after the dance. She said she wouldn't normally let me go to a grown-up dance, but since it was the minister's wife asking she guessed it would be okay.

Friday, November 19, 1943

At recess Betty and Lydia were discussing which movie to go to Saturday, and when they asked me what I wanted to see, I said, "I'm dreadfully sorry, but I have an engagement Saturday evening so I won't be able to go out in the afternoon."

"An engagement?" Betty asked.

"I'm going to a dance Saturday night," I said. I tried to sound bored, like Caroline does sometimes when she's talking about all the dances she goes to.

The bell rang just then, and I hurried in because I didn't want Betty and Lydia to know I was working at the dance, and with Nancy Goddard.

Nancy was at school today even though her brother was missing over at the war. She didn't look any different.

First let me say I am very busy and the night affords
no time for much writing because of no lights. This
weather is positively rotten, so wet and foggy and
keeps the spirits of a fellow pretty low.

Saturday, November 20, 1943
Afternoon

I am waiting for the dance to start and staying out of Mother's way, so I am writing in my diary. Mother is nervous today. We haven't heard from Alex over at the war for a while.

"I hope nothing's wrong," she said this morning at breakfast.

Dad put down the Saturday paper, took a bite of fried egg, and said, "He's fine. He's at the front now. Takes a while longer for mail to get through from up there."

"He probably doesn't have much time for writing anyway," Brian put in. He always talks with his mouth full of food and it looks totally disgusting. "He's probably busy shooting people."

Stephen went white hearing that, but it might have been a lump in the porridge. You expect porridge to be smooth and when you find a lump it makes your stomach *heave*, or at least it does mine.

"That's enough, Brian," Mother told him. She looked like she was thinking about giving him a smack on the head, then changed her mind and went to the stove. I was sweeping the floor at the time so I whacked Brian's leg with the broom for her. Doesn't he know that if Alex is shooting at people, people are probably shooting at Alex!

I pushed the broom over to the mat where everyone keeps their shoes and boots and started to take them off so I could shake it out. Mother is very particular that I do the whole floor, though I often point out to her that very few people look under our mat. Suddenly,

Mother shrieked, "Don't move Alex's boots!"

She made me jump right in the air. Everyone at the table stopped chewing and stared at her.

"Leave those boots alone until Alex comes back and moves them himself," she said.

She grabbed the broom out of my hand and pushed a cloth at me. "Go dust the dining room," she said.

"I already did," I told her. "Even the chair backs."

She stood silent a moment like she couldn't find any words to say, then pushed a bottle of lemon oil in my hand and said, "Well do it again. You never do a good job the first time anyway." Now my hands will stink of lemon oil all day. Mother is so unfair.

I better decide what I am wearing to the dance. I know I am working there, but what if a boy sees me and says, "May I have this dance?"

I'd say, "I'm sorry but I'm working." and I'd be very calm and firm, but he'd insist. "I don't care. I must dance with you," he'd say, and then he'd pick me up and lift me over the coat-check counter and right onto the dance floor. He'd look just like Rick Anderson.

I better make sure my underwear is decent just in case he wants to jitterbug. I've seen people jitterbug in movies, and the boys throw the girls up high and sometimes their panties show.

Saturday, November 20, 1943
Late at night—Nancy Goddard's house

Nancy lives in the manse right next to the church. It is a great advantage living so close, because she can leave one minute before church starts and still be there on time. It's a very big, old house. Cold too. Nancy and I are sharing a room. She booted her little sister out so I could have her bed.

The dance was wonderful even if I didn't get asked to jitterbug. I'll have lots to tell Betty and Lydia Monday. Nobody jitterbugged—maybe because the dance had a sign No ECCENTRIC DANCING ALLOWED at the entrance. Just as well—buttons don't hold panties as firmly as elastic used to.

At first I felt a bit awkward, because I didn't know whether or not to say anything to Nancy about her brother. Finally I said, "I'm sorry your brother is missing over at the war."

"No news is good news," she said. Then people started arriving and she took their money, and I took their coats and gave them a tag so they could get them back, and that's all she said about it.

There was one very funny moment when Caroline came in. She was holding on to an airman's arm, and laughing and smiling sweetly at him, when suddenly she saw me. Her eyes just about fell out of her head.

"What are you doing here?" she demanded.

"I'm working," I told her. "Do you want to check your coat?" I pride myself on the fact I sounded very businesslike.

"Does Mother know you're here?" asked Caroline, mad as a hornet.

"Mother has given her permission," I said *demurely*, though I really wanted to stick my tongue out at her.

Caroline's face was a picture. She grabbed the airman and pulled him away. There was no sweet smile now.

Nancy and I watched them dancing. "Your sister and her boyfriend dance really well," Nancy said.

"Her boyfriend?" I said.

"I thought that's what he was," Nancy said. "They come here most weekends. He's one of the Australian boys training at the Air Force base outside town."

I wonder if Mother knows. I didn't think about Caroline too much after that because the dance was so interesting. As it got later, some of the lights were turned off, softening the room, and the orchestra played slow songs. Nancy got us both some refreshments and coffee. Coffee is such a grown-up drink I forced it down, even though it tasted horrible.

It was very late when Rev. Goddard arrived to walk us back to the manse. The night was clear and cold and the stars shone bright. I said, "I wonder if the same stars shine over Alex in Italy?" Then I remembered Nancy's brother was missing and quickly added, "and Brent."

"God's eyes are watching over them all," Rev. Goddard said.

I like that thought.

Sunday, November 21, 1943

I helped Nancy in the nursery again, and this time I fed one of the babies from a bottle. It was a wonderful feeling holding such a tiny body. Nancy showed me how to burp him. If I burped that loud Mother would certainly have something to say, but a baby is allowed to burp, and the louder the better. I had lots to tell Alex in his letter today.

At supper I asked Caroline how her boyfriend was. I widened my eyes to look very innocent. Mother and Dad looked up quickly, exchanged glances then looked at Caroline.

"Fine," she mumbled and glared at me. She's going to get even with me for telling. That's why I am still sitting in the living room with Mother and Dad listening to Frank Sinatra on the radio and writing in my diary instead of in our room.

This year should see the end of the war and then we'll be back. You and the others will not have to write in those days, but for now asking you all to write.

Monday, November 22, 1943

A letter came from Alex over at the war. He says they'd hoped the war would be over by Christmas this year, but now it seems it might go a few months longer. He says he will definitely be home for next Christmas though. (I think he said that last year, too.)

Betty and Lydia were very interested in hearing all about the dance. They hung on my every word. Betty says she hoped I came in at a decent time, because Dorothy Dix says that if girls come sneaking in late they leave their characters behind them. I never told them I spent the night at Nancy's house.

Mrs. Ford said I'm not making much progress on my scarf. I don't much care.

Tuesday, November 23, 1943

Mother says I have to get supper started every Tuesday after school from now on, because she is volunteering at Smallman & Ingram's department store. They are holding "new clothes from old ones" workshops every Tuesday afternoon. "I've been taking skirt and pant hems up and down all my married life to make clothes stretch," she said. "Suddenly it's the thing to do, and I have to teach others how. I guess I was ahead of my time."

I decided to make pancakes. Pancakes, cinnamon toast, tomato soup and fried bologna are the only food we've cooked so far in school. Pancakes are good because, even if they're burned a bit, you can pour lots of syrup on them and they taste just fine.

At supper Brian flopped his pancake up and down on his plate and said, "These things weigh a ton. I think you've just invented a new weapon. We can feed these to the Germans and they won't be able to fight because their stomachs will be so heavy."

Dad said, "Just think, Bobby, you and your pancakes might win the war for us."

"Henry," Mother said. But I noticed her lips curving up a bit. They're all so mean.

Wednesday, November 24, 1943

Mother says Caroline has to bring her boyfriend home to introduce him to her and Dad. He's coming next Sunday.

> *I am writing this somewhere in Italy and believe me it is much colder than Sicily. Yesterday it snowed just like a Canadian flurry.*

Thursday, November 25, 1943

It snowed last night. I could tell as soon as I woke up because of the quiet. It's always like that with the first snow. *Muffled* snow sounds. It was like a white blanket covered our entire backyard. After school Stephen began making tracks for fox and goose. At first I didn't want to play with him, then he said I could be the fox, so I played.

The rules are the fox chases the goose all around the tracks and tries to catch him, but they can't go outside the tracks or they are out of the game. We made some safe places for the goose so Stephen could rest, because he's small. Brian came home from school, and he became the fox and Stephen and I were the geese, except Brian cheated by jumping over the tracks. Then Caroline got home from work and she began to chase us.

Suddenly we realized it was quite dark and wondered why Mother hadn't called us in to eat.

"You children were all playing so nicely," she said. "I thought supper could wait a while."

I can't believe she still thinks of me as a child.

Friday, November 26, 1943

In Domestic Arts class today, Mrs. Ford held up the blouse I was sewing and said, "Can anyone see a problem with this?"

I was so proud because I thought she'd seen how well I'd sewn it and was holding it up as an example. Then the girls started to giggle. I didn't understand what was wrong until Mrs. Ford said, "Where are you going to put your head, Roberta, now that you've sewn your sleeve to the neck?" She tossed it back on the table. "Get out your seam ripper," she said.

Even Betty and Lydia laughed. My face burned.

Saturday, November 27, 1943

Mother is making Caroline and me clean the house from top to bottom before Caroline's boyfriend comes. Even Stephen has to help by crawling under the dining room table and dusting its foot.

"I'm sure he's going to pull up the tablecloth and check for dirt underneath," I grumbled to Mother. "Besides, it's Caroline's boyfriend coming. Why do I have to clean?"

"It's your big mouth that's making him come here in the first place," Caroline hissed.

Brian grinned and piled his breakfast dishes in the sink and said, "Guess I'll go out and get away from all this woman work."

"Good idea," Dad said. "Go into the garage and you'll find some man's work waiting there. It needs a good sweeping." Brian looked quite *crestfallen.*

Sunday, November 28, 1943

Caroline fidgeted all through church until Mother glared at her. When we got home I telephoned Aunt Lily to tell her about Caroline's boyfriend coming. Aunt Lily said she'd be right over.

"Why don't you just phone up the whole world and tell them, Bobby?" Caroline yelled when she heard.

Caroline's boyfriend's name is James. He's from Australia and is at the Wings No. 4 AOS school training to be a navigator. He spoke so funny that Brian and I kept ducking into the kitchen and imitating his accent until we were falling down laughing. He's very tall and has really big hands. When Mother gave him a teacup, he got his finger stuck in the hole of the handle. Then he tried to pull it out and the handle broke off. He got very red in the face even though Mother told him never mind.

Dad kept going "Hmmph..." and then we'd all be quiet and wait for him to say something, but he never did.

Stephen was overwhelmed that he was in the same room as someone who flew planes, and couldn't stop looking at him.

When he left, Caroline, who'd been sweet as pie all afternoon, slammed the door and turned on us. "Well, that's just swell!" she shrieked. "Probably the most miserable afternoon he ever spent in his life." She grabbed my and Brian's arms and shook them hard. "You two laughing in the kitchen. And you, Dad, glowering at him all the time." Dad spluttered but he still didn't say anything. Caroline turned on Mother and Aunt Lily. "Did you have to give him the smallest teacup in the house?" Even Stephen didn't escape. "And you staring at him the whole time like you're a half-wit. He'll never come back again!" Then she burst into tears and ran out of the room.

"Well," Dad said.

Monday, November 29, 1943
Afternoon

I have an awful cold so I can't go to school. It's nice lying in bed hearing Mother tidying up downstairs. We listened to Mother's stories, *Front Line Family* and *Guiding Light*, on the radio. They were *heart-rending*. Mother listens to them every day. I wish I could stay home so I could listen to them, too. I just realized I don't have to go to knitting club today. If it weren't for my stuffy nose it'd be a near-perfect day.

Evening

Dad was listening to a war report on the radio and called us all in to listen. The man reporting was right there at the war. We could hear guns firing and bombs exploding. It was very noisy. Alex never did like a lot of noise.

Tuesday, November 30, 1943

When we got home Mother had Brian and me bring the Christmas decorations boxes up from the basement, but that was all. She won't let us put anything up for Christmas until December 1.

Dad said he heard there is a shipment of coal coming in from Alberta and he'll get some, but he is still worried that there won't be enough to get us through the winter. Most of the fuel goes to the war effort these days. "We'll have to watch what we use," he said, "because once it's gone, it's gone. Nothing like having to suffer chilblains to show I'm patriotic."

> *Last Sunday I was listening on the short wave to the hockey game between the Maple Leafs and Detroit. Foster Hewitt's voice still sounds the same as of old, very clear.*

Wednesday, December 1, 1943

A letter came from Alex over at the war. It was mailed just seven days ago and got here fast, because he sent it air mail. He says he heard the hockey game on the radio. It is strange that Alex can hear the same hockey game in Italy that Dad and the boys listened to in Canada. Mom dabbed tears from her eyes when she read that. Alex said they are planning a big Christmas dinner for them in Italy, but he doesn't know if he'll be on duty or not. He said they are short of men, because some got sick and some got wounded and some just left and never came back.

Dad says war "eats up men" and a lot of them are being conscripted. These are the men who didn't volunteer to go to join the armed forces in the first place, so the government is forcing them to join, except they don't have to go overseas to fight. Brian says they're called Zombies and that he'll volunteer as soon as he's done high school so people won't think him cowardly and call him a Zombie. Stephen hugged Mother. I don't know if Stephen would volunteer or not.

Thursday, December 2, 1943

I can't believe it. I am so excited my heart is pounding. My feet danced all the way home. Here is what happened:

Rick Anderson turned around in class and said, "Are you going to the movies on Saturday?"

At first I couldn't speak, then finally I was able to croak, "Maybe."

"Good movie playing. *Adventures of a Rookie*," Rick said. "Might see you there."

I have my first date!

Friday, December 3, 1943

Betty and Lydia asked me if I was going to the movies with them on Saturday, and I had to tell them I had a date with Rick Anderson.

Betty squealed and grabbed my arm. "What are you going to wear?" she asked.

"What if he wants to kiss you?" Lydia asked.

"She'll say no, of course," Betty told her. She pulled me ahead on the sidewalk, put her arm through mine, and made Lydia walk behind. Having a date automatically makes you the best friend, I guess.

"Now remember, Bobby, you don't kiss until you've gone out with the same boy four times, and you know his intentions are honourable," she said. "That's what Dorothy Dix says."

"Now, do you know how to make small talk?" she went on. "You have to know that for the first date to put the boy at ease, and wear gloves. My etiquette book says a girl should wear gloves on a date and shake hands with the boy with them on. Don't take them off."

"Even if I want to eat popcorn?" I asked. I'd think you'd have to take them off to eat popcorn or they'd get greasy.

She looked at me *pityingly.*

"My Mother says I can't date until I'm sixteen," Betty said, sighing hugely.

"Mine, too," Lydia agreed.

"You can't tell anyone," I told them. They both solemnly promised to never tell a soul.

"You are so lucky that your mother lets you date already," Betty went on, but she didn't make me feel like I was lucky. More like I was doing something wrong. I never thought to ask Mother if I could go on a date.

Saturday, December 4, 1943
Morning

This is the big day. I borrowed some of Caroline's Etiquette deodor-
ant cream, which I used liberally so I didn't smell if I got nervous. I
tried to pull my hair back from my face like Caroline wears hers, but
I couldn't get the hairpins to stay in. So I left it down. I don't want
hairpins falling out all over Rick Anderson. I wonder if he'll want to
hold my hand. I'd better borrow some of Caroline's hand cream so
they're soft. I'll put some on my lips, too, in case he kisses me, no
matter what Betty says.

Evening

I am never showing my face to the world again. Here is what happened:

When I came down for breakfast, Mother said, "I want you to
take Stephen to the Christmas Toytown at Smallman and Ingram's
so I can get some cleaning done in peace and quiet."

"But I'm going to the movies with Betty and Lydia," I protested.

"You can take Stephen with you then," she said.

"Betty and Lydia don't like little kids hanging around. Besides,
he'd find the show boring." I was feeling desperate now. I couldn't
take Stephen on my date. "Why can't Brian take him?"

"He's doing some work for Dad," Mother told me.

"Well, I'm not taking Stephen to the show," I announced.

"Very well then." Mother began to take off her apron. "I'll take
him to Toytown and the show, and you can do the cleaning."

I wanted to tell her about my date with Rick Anderson, but I was
scared she might say I couldn't go.

"Oh, all right," I grumbled. I grabbed my coat and hat. Maybe
Rick would like little kids.

"Put on your galoshes," Mother called. "It looks like it might snow."

Nobody wears galoshes on a date. I left them at home.

Toytown was pretty good with lots of decorations, though the toys were made from wood and cardboard because of the war. There's no metal to be found! Stephen wanted to stay longer but I made him leave, because I didn't want to be late for my date. When we came out of Smallman's it was snowing huge, wet flakes.

At the theatre I stood in front waiting for Rick. It was taking him a long time to come. Lydia and Betty were giggling and watching me, so I pretended to study the posters advertising the movie.

"Why aren't we going in?" Stephen asked.

"I'm waiting for someone," I told him. I still hadn't figured out how to make him not tell Mother about my date.

Finally I saw Rick Anderson coming down the street with a bunch of his friends. I put a big smile on my face and stepped out, but they pushed right past me like they didn't even see me.

I said, "Hi Rick."

He turned his head quickly and mumbled, "Yeah, hi." He didn't even say my name.

Betty and Lydia were standing in line watching, so I kept the big smile on my face and told them, "We decided to go another time because his friends wanted him to go with them."

I don't think they believed me. I wouldn't have believed me. I looked at the poster again. "I don't think this movie is suitable for a young child." I grabbed Stephen's hand and walked away. I tried so hard to keep the tears in my eyes, where they belong, that my face felt like wood by the time I got home. My feet were lumps of ice and my shoes water-stained.

"Why aren't you at the movies?" Mother said.

"I have a sick stomach," I told her and went upstairs, taking my ruined shoes with me so Mother wouldn't see.

Thank goodness only Betty and Lydia know about Rick Anderson, and they're my friends so they won't tell anyone.

> *I had a letter from Stan. I hope they don't transfer*
> *him to the infantry because all the infantry has to*
> *offer is blood and guts.*

Sunday, December 5, 1943

I told Mother my stomach was still not feeling well, so she let me stay home from Sunday school and church. I stayed in my room most the day reading, except when Mother insisted I help make Christmas pudding. It's snowing hard outside and the wind keeps rattling the window.

> *I have half a dozen blankets as well as canvas to*
> *cover me at night and this is quite warm. The only*
> *thing missing is a fire to crowd around.*

Monday, December 6, 1943

A horrible day! I didn't even go to knitting club, I was so upset. Here is what happened:

I hung my coat up in the cloakroom and walked into class and sat at my desk and took out my books. Suddenly, I realized how quiet it was and saw everyone was looking at me without really looking at me, and poking each other and giggling. I turned in my seat and Rick Anderson was standing at the back of the classroom with four other boys who immediately burst out laughing. Rick looked very uncomfortable and then it hit me. They all knew about my date with Rick Anderson. They all knew I liked him—even Rick!

Someone told. But the only people who knew were Betty and Lydia and they're my best friends and they solemnly swore.

Brian just came in. He poked around Caroline's dresser for a few minutes, so I said, "What are you looking for?" It came out kind of muffled, because I was trying to keep my head in my diary so he wouldn't see I was crying.

"Nothing. Just looking." Then he went and stood looking out the window. "Do you want me to punch out Rick Anderson for you?" he asked suddenly.

I couldn't believe it. "You know about that?" I shrieked. "You don't even go to my school and you know about that?"

He shrugged. "Word gets around. So do you want me to or not?"

"Punch him?" I shook my head. "It's not really his fault," I said, though it might make me feel better if Brian did punch him.

I am utterly *humiliated*.

Tuesday, December 7, 1943

Caroline looked positively green this morning. "You must have the flu," I told her. "Lots of kids at school have got it."

She swallowed hard and said, "I guess so."

Betty and Lydia were not waiting for me at the end of the street, so I walked to school alone. When I got there, Betty said, "My father gave us a ride on his way to work."

I waited all day, my stomach in one huge knot, but no one said anything about Rick Anderson.

"A seven-day-wonder forgotten in one day," Nancy whispered to me in class.

I made cinnamon toast and tomato soup for supper. Stephen said it was his favourite meal ever.

Wednesday, December 8, 1943

It is slushy and cold today. I couldn't stop shivering at recess, which made me think about Alex over in Italy. Maybe he's cold, too. I worked on the scarf for the soldiers after school until bedtime. I dropped a couple of stitches, but Mother found them for me. I stayed up later than usual to finish it. Mother didn't say anything.

Thursday, December 9, 1943

Mrs. Ford was surprised that my scarf was done. "You've been very industrious, Roberta."

What surprised me was that she put her arm around my shoulders. "It is lovely and thick. It will certainly keep some soldier warm this winter."

I felt like someone had lit a fire in my toes and it spread through my whole body.

> *I do not get my full quota of rest and sleep—always*
> *on the move, however we take it all in good spirits. I*
> *am always glad to hear our artillery shells over head.*

Friday, December 10, 1943

School's out in twelve days for Christmas holidays.

Saturday, December 11, 1943

Today is Caroline's nineteenth birthday. It was very strange though; she tried to smile but it looked wobbly. Mother kept glancing at her and frowning until Caroline jumped to her feet and said, "Bobby, I know it's my birthday, but I am going to treat you to the show."

Betty and Lydia were at the movies and seemed quite surprised to see me there with Caroline. I was surprised to see them. I said, "You didn't say you were going to the show."

"We thought maybe you might not want to go to the movies with everything that happened and all. You know—Rick?" Betty whispered. I don't know why she was whispering.

At the show Caroline lit up a cigarette. I didn't even know she smoked. It must be lovely to be nineteen.

Sunday, December 12, 1943

I didn't mind Sunday school or church today. I love singing Christmas carols. My favourite is "Angels We Have Heard on High." Tonight is the Christmas play. Stephen is a shepherd. He's wearing Dad's old housecoat and a towel on his head. Brian said, "You look like you're on your way to the bathtub."

Mother says we all have to go, even Caroline. I have to write my letters to Alex and Uncle Billy now.

Monday, December 13, 1943

I'm trying to think of a wonderful Christmas present I can get for Betty that would be suitable for a best friend. She is having a "little party" (that's what she called it, not me) next week, but I noticed it is in the *Social and Personal* column in the paper as a tea for the "not-out" set. Betty has noticed that Nancy Goddard keeps coming to talk to me. "I guess you're friends with Nancy Goddard now and won't have time to come to my party," she said.

I was terrified she'd not invite me, so I assured her I wasn't Nancy's friend and that I had a very nice present for her. I have to go to Betty's party. I've never been to a party that was in the paper before. I didn't even know I was in the "not-out" set.

Lydia said, "Betty has really hurt feelings. She's very sensitive."

I have to find Betty a really good present to make it crystal clear to her that she is my best friend. Problem is there's so many people in my family to buy for I'm afraid I'll run out of money before it's her turn. Mother says I should just make her a card. "Why spend good money on someone who has everything?" she said. She obviously doesn't understand about Betty's hurt feelings.

The streets are full of barefoot people, dirty and in rags, mule carts and begging children, women walking down the streets with pots, hay and chickens on their heads.

Tuesday, December 14, 1943

Finally, a letter came from Alex over at the war. It was dated October 30, 1943. He sent us some pictures showing two volcanic mountains in Sicily and a small boy carrying a huge bag of sand twice his own size on his head. My favourites are the ones with Alex, sitting or standing with his chums. They always have their arms around each other so they must be good friends. Mother says he looks a bit thin to her, but Dad said, "Rubbish! He's fine."

As always, Alex asked us to send him cigarettes.

Wednesday, December 15, 1943

Every morning this week the school gathers in the gymnasium and sings carols, except the boys. They won't sing. Caroline's boyfriend came over tonight to pick her up, but Caroline rushed him right out the door before we had a chance to say hello. I guess she doesn't want us laughing or staring at him. It got quite mild and all the snow is gone. I hope it snows for Christmas. Still don't know what to get Betty.

Thursday, December 16, 1943

This is the last day of the knitting club before Christmas holidays. Mrs. Ford said I could graduate to socks in the new year. She brought us all some cookies to eat and told us we all did a wonderful job supporting "our boys overseas." Mrs. Ford also said she wouldn't be back after the holidays because she was starting a family, but hoped we would keep meeting as our work was vital to the war effort. That made me feel quite important.

It gets dark so early these days, it was nearly black by the time I walked home. No one turns their house lights on because of the power shortage due to the factories working all hours. I tripped on the sidewalk and stubbed my toe, which is still hurting. I wonder what it's like in England during a blackout. Mother made blackout curtains a couple of years ago when the war first started, but we never did have to use them. I bet in England my feet would be black and blue all over.

Friday, December 17, 1943

Nancy Goddard's brother is no longer listed as missing—he's a prisoner of war. Mother helps pack parcels for prisoners of war at the POW Parcel Center, as she said our boys were very hard up for food in the prison camps overseas and in *"dire straits."* Baby-sat the little monsters down the street for extra money for Christmas gifts.

> *I hope you all have a very good Christmas this year.*
> *I sure would like to be there and have the day at*
> *home and sit down to a very rare dinner of turkey,*
> *cranberry sauce, cake or pudding and these days my*
> *mind goes back to the good old days and the Xmas's*
> *we used to have.*

Saturday, December 18, 1943

We went and got our Christmas tree today. Brian said, "We should go and chop our tree down in the woods like lumberjacks."

Dad said, "We'll just buy it, like city folk."

It's a perfect tree. Much better than last year's, which had half the back missing. Dad put the lights on first, then we put the balls and ornaments on. Aunt Lily came over and helped. Brian threw fistfuls of tinsel on it so it sat in huge, silver clumps on the branches. He said it was a much faster way to decorate a tree. He ruins everything.

After the tree was decorated, we had an early supper and went to Dad's work for the children's party. We each got a net stocking with an orange, a candy cane, a whistle, and mine had a tiny, sweet doll with a baby bottle. I'm too old for dolls but I kept it anyway. Caroline went to a dance with James instead of the party.

Brian said, "This is the last year I'm coming to this thing. It's so boring." He ate all his candy in one big mouthful so his cheeks bulged, and put his empty stocking on Stephen's head and called him "Alf the Elf." Brian is so stupid.

Sunday, December 19, 1943

Five days until Christmas! At church today, Rev. Goddard said we should search our hearts for charity and forgiveness. He said we should try to forgive our enemies. I wonder if he means the Germans, too. Even the ones who took his son prisoner. I wonder if Alex forgives his enemies, who are right near him. I don't think I could have charity and forgiveness in my heart when someone was shooting at me.

Caroline's boyfriend came to supper tonight. Aunt Lily and Grandma came, too. Grandma said, "That was not a very good sermon today. Rev. Goddard should concentrate more on his preaching and less on adding to his family. Eight children, another on the way."

"Mother!" said Mother.

Dad and James laughed.

I never noticed that Mrs. Goddard was having a baby. Nancy must know how it happens.

Monday, December 20, 1943

I'm trying to figure out how to save money for Betty's present. I have $2.25. I didn't even go to the show last Saturday to save myself 25 cents. I have to give 25 cents at school for the War Bond Book, so I really only have $2.00. I figure if I bought Mother and Dad's present together that would save me a bit. Too bad I didn't knit faster. I could have made everyone scarves. I think I'll write Grandma a poem and put it in a card and that'll save me money, too; besides, it's much more personal than a bought gift. I don't know what to buy for Betty.

It should be gratifying for you to hear that after eight months your Xmas parcel arrived.

Winter 1943/44

Today was the last day of school, but I couldn't even be happy because Betty's party is tomorrow and I still don't have her present!

Caroline came in and said, "Why so glum, chum?" I explained about Betty and she snorted and said, "Some friend."

She went into the closet and came back with a beautiful red chiffon scarf. She tossed it to me and said, "Give her this. I don't need it any more. After all, we don't want you friendless, because then you'd be hanging around me all the time."

I ironed the scarf until every wrinkle was gone. It is an absolutely perfect gift for Betty. Very elegant.

I got my period. I can't believe I have to have this every single month!

Today was Betty's party. I almost didn't go. Here's what happened:

Just before I left, Mother said, "Brian will come at 6:30 to walk you home."

"Walk me home?" I was furious. "I'm perfectly able to walk home myself."

"It gets dark early these days. A girl does not walk in the dark by herself," Mother said. "Brian will walk you home or you won't go."

Brian looked just as mad as me. "I'm not walking her home."

"Yes you are," Mother said, and her voice meant it. "After cadets, you stop at Betty's."

"You're not to come to the house!" I yelled at him. "You're to stay on the driveway."

"What makes you think I want to come to a party with dumb, giggly girls?" Brian sneered.

"Just shut up!" I told him.

"That's enough of that language," Mother said. "Or you won't be going to any party."

As always, Brian nearly ruined everything.

There were six girls at Betty's party, even Nancy Goddard!

"Her brother is a prisoner of war," Betty explained.

Betty's mother had made tiny little sandwiches in diamond shapes and cut all the crusts off the bread. Stephen would have liked that because he hates crusts. Mother would have thought it a dreadful waste, but I thought them so beautiful they made me sigh every time I ate one. We had ruby-coloured punch in glass cups! If you turned the cup and caught the light just a certain way, it was like staring at a tiny rainbow. I love everything about Betty's house.

I gave Betty the red scarf and she was very impressed. There was just one sticky moment when she asked me where I got it. I didn't know what to say, but Nancy Goddard said, "I saw some scarves like those in Jackson's Ladies' Wear."

"Yes, that's where it came from," I said quickly. I hope that is one of those lies that are more like fibs than lies. I'm so lucky Nancy saw the same scarf at Jackson's.

"It looks beautiful with your hair, Betty," Lydia said.

Everyone there thought it a wonderful present. Betty put her arm through mine and sat beside me for the rest of the party.

At 6:40 the doorbell rang. I had forgotten about Brian! Betty's mother invited him in and gave him a cookie and a glass of punch. At first I was horrified. I thought he'd ruin everything, but Brian spoke very politely to Betty and her mother. He told them how he was studying aircraft recognition at cadets, so he'd know if we were being attacked by German airplanes or our own. He almost sounded interesting.

Betty said, "You look very handsome in your uniform." I thought Brian's ears would burst into flame, they turned so red.

When I left I told Betty's mother it was the most *gracious* party I'd ever attended.

On the way home Brian kept repeating, "It was the most gracious party I've ever attended." Finally, I said, "You look very handsome in your uniform."

That shut him up.

Thursday, December 23, 1943

Two days until Christmas. Stephen and I took some of Dad's freshly washed socks right off the stretcher so they would be nice and big to hold all the stuff we'll get. Clean, too.

Friday, December 24, 1943

It's very late and quiet. Even Caroline is sleeping. I am the only person awake in the whole wide world. It's snowing! I am sitting beside the window writing, using just the soft light from the snow to see by. I tiptoed downstairs a few minutes ago and our stockings are full to the brim, and there's lot of presents under the tree. Tomorrow is going to be absolutely perfect.

> *For us now has passed Xmas 1943. Three days of*
> *revelry and such as I've never seen and these boys*
> *knew or had that feeling this may be the last.*

Saturday, December 25, 1943
Night

I'm sleeping with Caroline in her bed, though we're not really sleeping. Caroline's mostly crying. I can't, though my eyes very badly want to. It has been a dreadful day. Here is what happened:

Christmas Day started out perfect just like I knew it would. We woke up real early, though Caroline complained about having to get out of bed at such an *unholy* hour. We emptied our stockings, then had breakfast. Mother said we had to wait for Aunt Lily to bring Grandma before we could open the presents under the tree.

Later, Dad and Mother and Aunt Lily all had some eggnog with rum, though Grandma said it was the devil's drink.

"Well," Dad said as he emptied his cup. "I'll say this for the devil. He makes a mighty fine drink."

We were sitting down for supper in the dining room, all wearing our paper party hats. Dad began to carve the turkey when the doorbell rang. Mother went to the door and walked back smiling. "It's a telegram from overseas, Lily. Probably Billy and Alex wishing us Merry Christmas."

Alex had sent a telegram last year at Christmas and another for Mother's birthday.

Mother opened the telegram, and her smile slowly faded. She went very white and began to slump. Dad jumped up, caught her and set her in a chair.

"Get a glass of water for your mother, Brian!" he yelled.

Aunt Lily grabbed the telegram from Mother's hand and read it, then crumpled the paper into a ball and threw it on the hall floor. She put on her coat and went out, leaving the door wide open.

"What on earth..." Grandma hurried over and smoothed out the telegram.

"The Department of National Defence regrets..." she began, then, "Good Lord in Heaven," she said. "Good Lord in Heaven. William is dead and Alex is wounded. Good Lord. Good Lord. Good Lord!" Her voice sailed up into a wail at the last Lord.

"Caroline, help with your grandma," Dad ordered. "Bobby, find out where your Aunt Lily's gone. Brian, where the hell's that water?"

I stared at Dad. I couldn't hear what he said, only Grandma howling, "Good Lord."

"Now, Bobby. Go!" Dad's voice cracked.

I ran out the door and I looked up and down the street, but I couldn't see Aunt Lily. Her car was still in front of the house, so I knew she was walking.

Mrs. Turner came out onto her front porch, knife and fork in hand, her husband close behind. "I saw the telegram boy. Is it bad news?"

She didn't wait for my answer but hurried off to our house. I ran to the end of the block and saw Aunt Lily rapidly walking to her house. I ran after her. Aunt Lily went right into the backyard, threw herself on her hands and knees and began ripping out her mums and roses. She scared me so badly I didn't know what to do so I just watched. Then I realized her fingers were bleeding from the thorns. I grabbed one of her arms and yanked.

"Stop! Please stop, Aunt Lily."

She pushed me off. "Why try to keep something beautiful in a war?" she said. "It only gets destroyed. Billy will never see it again, so what does it matter?"

I tried to pull her back again, and this time she threw back her hand and hit me hard across the side of my head. I fell and couldn't see anything except black and white spots for a few seconds, then

Aunt Lily was holding me and crying, "I'm so sorry, Bobby. I'm so sorry."

I took Aunt Lily in the house, or she took me, I don't know which. I helped her out of her coat and sat her in a chair. I thought she might want to wash her cut hands, but she sat in the chair wringing them and rocking back and forth. I sat opposite her and watched her until Brian came. Then he sat with me and we both watched her and after a long time Mother and Dad and Grandma came and told us to go home.

On my way out I stopped in the garden. Rose bushes lay on their sides, browned petals crushed into the mud. Aunt Lily and I must have still had our party hats on, because little bits of paper stained the snow green and gold.

Dad opened the back door and yellow light fell across the garden in a wide beam to the back fence, and I saw red blossoms like blood beaded on the white snow. I went over and tore them completely to bits.

"What are you doing?" Brian asked.

"Getting rid of these," I said. "They're horrible. They're called love-lies-bleeding. They killed Uncle Billy."

Friday, December 31, 1943

It's New Year's Eve. Mother has been staying with Aunt Lily. Caroline and I are supposed to be making supper while she's gone, but Caroline gets sick every time she looks at food so we've been eating a lot of pancakes, cinnamon toast and tomato soup. Nobody seems to care. I just remembered: Mother gave me a brand new diary for Christmas, but it doesn't feel proper to write in it so I'm still using my old notebook. Brian gave me the wooden box Dad said he had to make to keep my diary in, and it has a little padlock and key.

I'm not staying up until midnight. I don't care about the new year.

Some of my chums when we were in Canada together, and have a photo of several of them in my album at home, were killed in the raid.

Monday, January 3, 1944

School started but we didn't go, because Uncle Billy's memorial service was today. The church was very full. In front of the altar, there was a picture of Uncle Billy in his army uniform and flowers all around it. Alex and Uncle Billy both had their pictures in the newspaper today.

Dad found out that Alex and Uncle Billy were hit in a mortar attack. Alex got two pieces of shrapnel in his leg and a broken arm. He won't be going back to the war. He'll be coming home in a few months. Uncle Billy won't.

Aunt Lily cried through the service and told Mother, "I don't even have his body to bury. They can't even send me his body. He's over there in a grave in some damned forsaken country. I don't even know where he's buried."

I thought a really horrible thing in church during the memorial service. So horrible I can barely write it here. I thought, thank goodness it was Uncle Billy who was killed and not Alex. I hope God doesn't punish me for thinking that. I couldn't help it. It just happened.

Tuesday, January 4, 1944

Caroline was sick this morning and couldn't go to work. Mother came in our room and said, "Get to school, Bobby."

"It's not time yet," I told her.

"I don't care. Get to school. Now."

When I got home Mother was putting on her hat and coat.

"Are you going to the old clothes workshop?" I asked.

"The old clothes workshop!" She stopped with her hat pin in her hand and turned to me. Angry red spots appeared high on her cheeks.

"Well, it's Tuesday," I said quickly. Mother was scaring me, she looked so mad.

"Billy is dead. Lily is falling apart. Alex is wounded. Your sister..." She clamped her lips together with a snap, then opened them again. "And you think I'm going to the old clothes workshop!" She came toward me with her hand in the air to smack me. Then stopped, whirled about, jabbed her pin into her hat and grabbed her purse. The clasp gave way and all the ration books flew out and slid across the floor. "Damn this war! I'm sick of it!" Mother yelled. I have never, ever heard Mother swear before.

Wednesday, January 5, 1944

The house is full of whispers today. No one is talking out loud. Not even me and I don't know why. I hate our house today. I keep waking up in the night to find Stephen sleeping beside me.

Thursday, January 6, 1944

Our Christmas tree is still up. Mother usually takes it down on New Year's Day.

Friday, January 7, 1944

A letter came from Alex over at the war, except it wasn't really from Alex. Someone else wrote the letter to say Alex was fine and he hoped we all were fine. It didn't sound one bit like Alex. Our house is so quiet my stomach hurts.

Saturday, January 8, 1944

I was on my way to Betty's house when Mother said I couldn't go. "I want to talk to you, Roberta." She took a deep breath and said in one big rush, "Your sister is having a baby. It will become very apparent in the near future as she gets...gets bigger, so I am telling you now. Your father is telling the boys." And she left to see Aunt Lily.

I went upstairs, and Caroline was lying on her bed smoking a cigarette and staring at the ceiling.

"Mother's gone out," I said.

Caroline said nothing.

"You're not married," I said.

"What?"

"Mother said you were having a baby but you're not married."

Caroline rolled all over her bed laughing.

Sunday, January 9, 1944

At supper Caroline asked Dad if he wanted some more potatoes, but he wouldn't answer her.

Caroline repeated, "Dad, do you want more potatoes?"

But he still wouldn't look at or talk to her.

Caroline burst into tears and ran up the stairs and locked herself in our bedroom.

Brian didn't come home until after supper. Dad asked, "Where have you been?"

"Out," Brian said.

Dad started yelling at him and I went into the living room and turned on the radio, loud.

Later I went into the garage where Dad was. He had taken the tires off the car and put it on blocks. "No gas to run it. The tires are shot and there's no rubber for new ones. It can rot there for all I care," he said. "Go to bed, Bobby."

"I can't," I told him. "Caroline won't let me in the bedroom."

"Go sleep in Stephen's room, then."

"The needles are all falling off the Christmas tree," I told him.

The Germans have taken most everything the French have, even the girls and men for slave labour.

Spring 1944

I'm writing in my diary again, though I'm still using the old note-book. I don't feel happy enough to use the new one I got for Christmas. It doesn't seem proper somehow.

Caroline moved in with Aunt Lily. Mother said it was to keep Aunt Lily company, but I think it was mostly because Caroline isn't Dad's favourite any more.

One night she yelled at Dad, "Look at me! Why won't you look at me?" Dad said nothing, so Caroline packed her bags and left. I always thought I wanted my own room, but I don't.

Betty and Lydia aren't my best friends any more. Here is how it happened: I was sitting on the bench in the cloakroom pulling off my boots, and coats hung all around hiding me so Betty and Lydia didn't know I was there. Betty was whispering to some of the other girls about Caroline and I heard her say, "...fallen woman, that's what Dorothy Dix would call her."

I stood up then and Betty saw me and her face was quite a picture, but I suspect mine was worse. The other girls sort of melted away into the classroom, but Betty didn't move. I wanted to run away right then, but I was afraid I'd get in trouble if I left school, so instead I walked right by her like she didn't exist. I held my eyes wide all day so they wouldn't cry. For some reason my jaw ached for two days after, even though it was my eyes I held open.

Wednesday, March 22, 1944

Alex is coming home in two days. Well, not really home. He has to stay in Westminster Hospital. I thought that would make Mother and Dad happy, but Dad is still quiet and Mother is still touchy all the time. Everything feels wrong here. Even Brian doesn't tease me any more.

Thursday, March 23, 1944

Caroline came to our house tonight for the first time in a month. James was with her. They stood in the living room and Caroline said, "James and I got married this morning at City Hall." Then she started to cry and Mother started to cry.

James said, "I love Caroline and I will take care of her. She'll be getting my pay while I'm away."

Dad got up and went out to the garage. Then I started to cry. James stood twisting his hat around and around in his hand, looking utterly miserable for someone newly married.

Friday, March 24, 1944

I'm writing this at the kitchen table. Mother and Dad went to meet Alex's train, and then they'll go to the hospital to see him settled in. He came over by hospital ship.

Stephen is at the other end of the table doing his spelling homework and bothering me with questions.

"What do you think Alex looks like now?" he asked.

"Like Alex," I told him. "Who do you think he'll look like?"

"I don't know," Stephen said. "I don't remember him very well."

"You've seen his pictures," I pointed out.

"They're just pictures," Stephen said. "Not really him." He went back to his spelling.

I started to worry then that I wouldn't remember what Alex looked like, so I got the pictures he sent us from over at the war just to be sure. I never noticed before, but in all the pictures of Alex and his army friends they always have their arms around each other's shoulders. I don't remember Alex doing that when he lived here.

The Catania battlefield—wrecked German and
Italian planes, tanks, strew the roadside. On the
walls of buildings one can see here and there where
there were once pictures of Mussolini, Goebbels and
Hitler.

Saturday, March 25, 1944

"Alex seems to be settling in quite well," Mother told us at supper.

"Why does he have to stay at the hospital?" Stephen asked.

"His leg's not entirely healed," Mother said.

"Well, when will it be better so he can come home?" Stephen asked.

"Heavens, Stephen, I'm not a doctor. I don't know. Stop asking so many questions," Mother scolded.

She got up very quickly and went to the kitchen sink and ran the tap rinsing plates. Her face looked like mine does when I fib.

Sunday, March 26, 1944

Church and Sunday school. It seems odd that church and Sunday school haven't changed. Everything else has. We sing "Holy, Holy, Holy" at the beginning of every service, do the readings, listen to the sermon, give the offering, then the minister prays the benediction and we leave. It never changes.

It feels very strange to not write letters to Alex and Uncle Billy at the war any more. Sunday afternoon doesn't feel right without the letters, and sometimes I don't know what to do with the time.

Mother and Dad went to see Alex this afternoon. I think there is something terribly wrong with him that Mother isn't telling us. Maybe Alex had his leg amputated. I bet that is what really happened and Mother is afraid to tell us.

Monday, March 27, 1944

Mother says I am to go to see Alex at the hospital tomorrow after school, because she is going back to the making new clothes from old ones workshop and someone should visit him.

"You must remember, Bobby," Mother said, "Alex has been through a terrible time." She looked uncertain, as if she couldn't remember what she wanted to say, then, "He sometimes doesn't feel like talking, so you just sit with him and keep him company. Read to him if you like."

I'm very scared because I know Alex doesn't have a leg and Mother just can't tell me.

Tuesday, March 28, 1944

I went with Rev. Goddard and Nancy to the hospital after school. Nancy does volunteer work there. The sun shone today, a watery, pale yellow, but warm enough to leave brown grass holes in the white snow. I undid my winter coat. If Mother had been there she would tell me to do it up because I'd catch a chill. It wouldn't matter if it's as hot as a summer day. If it's March or April, Mother insists your coat be done up.

Rev. Goddard introduced me to a nurse and left. She said I'd find Alex in a sunroom and pointed down a long corridor. Nancy said she was late to help with preparing the afternoon drinks, so she left. I looked down the corridor for a bit, then went back outside.

Melting snow rivers ran down the sides of the road. I put a browned leaf boat in one stream and watched it sail through a snow tunnel and out the other side. It was so interesting I did it again and again.

The breeze smelled today. In the winter, air doesn't have much scent, but today it smelled like melting and Spring. I sailed leaves for so long, Rev. Goddard and Nancy came out and said it was time to go, so I never did get to visit Alex.

Wednesday, March 29, 1944

Mother found out today I didn't see Alex. "What on earth possessed you to go all that way, then not go in?" she said.

I just shrugged. She's making me go back Saturday.

Thursday, March 30, 1944

I don't want to go back to the hospital.

Friday, March 31, 1944

It's Good Friday so there's no school. Grandma and Aunt Lily came to supper, though Grandma said our time would have been better spent in prayer. Dad offered to take her to the church and leave her there so she could pray, but he sounded more mad than funny.

"James left for Halifax yesterday," Aunt Lily said. "And then he'll be sent overseas. Caroline's quite upset about it."

"Why on earth didn't she say something?" Mother said. "We could have seen him off."

Aunt Lily looked quickly at Dad and then away. "I think they just wanted the remaining time to themselves," she said.

Well I'm seeing plenty of war these days and the
bitter and sweet of it. When you send your next letter

please put some flints in the envelope because we
can't get any here and matches are as scarce as
blazes.

Saturday, April 1, 1944

Hospitals smell horrible and they are too quiet. The nurses' shoes make no noise, and the only way you know they're around is the rustling of their starched aprons. People in hospitals talk in low murmurs that make me think of sick people. I had to ask a nurse for directions to Alex's room and she said quite impatiently, "Speak up! I can't hear you." She didn't have to get huffy. I thought I was supposed to be quiet like them.

I walked down white-walled corridors forever to find Alex. I felt maybe I should leave a trail of breadcrumbs, like Hansel and Gretel, to find my way back or I'd be lost. It smelled dreadful, like medicine and operations. My hair still smells like it.

I went past one room and a man was shouting. I stopped and wondered if I should tell a nurse, but another man walking down the hall said, "Don't worry about him. He does that all the time. Never shuts up for a moment."

Finally I found Alex at the end of a corridor in a sunroom. At first all I could see was a lot of men, some playing cards, some reading, and one man was playing a piano. Then I saw a man sitting in a wheelchair looking out the window, and even from the back of his head I knew it was Alex. My heart pounded. Mother and Dad had said Alex was home, but I never really believed it until that moment. The first thing I did was look down at Alex's feet, and there they were tucked inside slippers. Both of them!

I ran over to him and stood in front of his chair. "Alex, you're really here."

He looked at me, but he didn't say anything even when I shook his shoulder and said his name again.

"Alex, what's wrong?" I said. "It's me, Bobby." I was getting scared.

"Don't bother yourself, sweetie." One of the men looked up from his cards. "He never speaks to any one. Sits all day in front of that window, poor bastard."

I shook his arm again, then bent and looked into his eyes, then tumbled over onto my backside in shock. Alex's eyes were empty. Empty. Just thinking about his eyes now while I write this makes me shake all over. Alex's body might be back from the war, but he's still over there.

I ran out of the sunroom and right out of the hospital. I was crying so hard my face was swimming in tears and I couldn't breathe. I thought I heard someone calling my name, but I just kept running. I didn't even wait for Rev. Goddard to take me home. I saw a bus and hopped right on. I realized afterwards it could have been going anywhere, but it wasn't and I got home. Where's my Alex?

Sunday, April 2, 1944

Easter Sunday. I got new white gloves to wear to church. Mother hid eggs for us, but Brian wouldn't hunt for them because he said he was too old. I said, "Good. All the more for Stephen and me." But I didn't really mean it.

After church I went to Aunt Lily's to see Caroline. She doesn't come to church much any more, especially since Mother and Dad can't make her. Aunt Lily was out visiting Grandma.

"What are you doing here?" Caroline asked. She sounded snappish, like she used to when we shared a bedroom, and for some reason that made me feel quite cheery.

Then she sighed and got very teary. "I'm sorry, Bobby. I'm not feeling too well today. If you don't mind, I think I'll go lie down." That did not sound anything like the old Caroline, and my heart sank. I hate the way I feel right now. It's like there's this heavy grey blanket covering me, and no matter what I do I can't push it aside.

I went into Aunt Lily's garden. I remembered how she'd pulled up all the flowers and hit me, though accidentally, on Christmas Day. Nothing has been touched in the garden since then. I pulled out a dead plant near my foot, then another, and then I went into the basement and got a rake and hoe and began to smooth lumps from the dirt.

"What are you doing?" Aunt Lily nearly made me jump out of my skin, she came up behind me so quietly.

"Fixing your garden so you can plant it," I told her.

She looked at it, then said, "I haven't time to do any gardening this year with my job and all." Her voice reminded me of Alex's eyes. Empty.

"Can I?" I asked.

"I don't care," she said and walked into the house.

Monday, April 3, 1944

Easter Monday, so I didn't have to go to school. Normally I like being out of school, but with no friends and everyone acting strangely, I almost wished I was at school. Almost.

My training bra has been pinching me dreadfully for a couple of weeks now. I went downstairs to find Mother to tell her I needed a new one. She was sitting in a chair darning a sock. Dad was reading the newspaper.

"What's wrong with Alex?" I asked Mother. I meant to tell her about my bra, so that question surprised me as much as her.

Dad's newspaper lowered a bit, and I knew he was listening, though his face was still covered.

Mother put down the sock, sighed, then said, "It's called combat exhaustion. He's in shock, but the doctors are sure it will wear off in time and he'll begin to respond more. I'd hoped if he saw you it might help. You two were always close." She picked up the sock, then stared at the needle in her hand like she didn't know what to do with it. Dad turned the page of the newspaper. I never did tell Mother my bra was too tight.

Naples is the most wrecked city I've ever seen and was once one of the most beautiful cities in the world.

Tuesday, April 4, 1944

Nancy caught up with me on the way home from school.

"Why did you run away from the hospital? Dad and I were worried."

I shrugged. I didn't feel much like talking to Nancy but didn't know how to get rid of her.

"I was pretty scared going there at first," Nancy said. "But you get used to it and the people are really nice."

I can't believe Nancy works in that place.

For some reason I feel better that she was scared, too, but I'm never going back.

"Mrs. Ford had her baby," she told me. "She had a boy."

I figured it was now or never. "Nancy, how are babies made?"

Her eyes went quite wide. "You don't know how babies are made?"

"If I knew, I wouldn't have to ask you, would I?" I pointed out.

And she told me. It is so disgusting I cannot even write it here. I cannot begin to imagine Mother and Dad doing *that* even though Nancy pointed out they must have, because I'm here and so are Alex, Caroline, Brian and Stephen. Nancy must have got it wrong.

Wednesday, April 5, 1944

I went and saw Caroline after school today. She doesn't work any more since she's married because, Mother says, "she's showing." I had no idea you couldn't work once your stomach showed you were having a baby.

"I know how babies are made," I announced. I was hoping to get a clue that Nancy was wrong.

"Good for you. Bet Mother never told you." Caroline laughed. When she did, I realized that Caroline doesn't laugh too much any more. She always had a nice laugh.

"It's perfectly dreadful," I said, watching her closely.

"It's not dreadful," she told me. "If it's with someone you love it's wonderful. You'll find out some day."

"I seriously doubt it. I will never do *that* with anyone," I insisted.

I started to go out to the garden when Caroline asked, "How is Dad?"

"He's fine," I told her.

"Good," she said. I thought she was going to say more, but she didn't.

Thursday, April 6, 1944

I wore my coat to school in the morning, but it was so warm when I walked home after school I had to carry it. The maples have buds on them though our chestnut tree doesn't yet. I suddenly had the urge to work in Aunt Lily's garden. The crocuses are up and some of the daffodils are pushing green shoots through the dirt. The ground felt very warm to my fingers, but just on top. It was still cold underneath. I never had a whole garden to plan out myself. I took some paper and drew a picture of Aunt Lily's backyard and what I would put in it. I am going to replant some of Aunt Lily's roses that she pulled out, and I am going to put in some vegetables for Aunt Lily and Caroline and the new baby. I'll borrow some of Dad's lettuce and bean seeds. For some reason looking at the brown earth and the daffodils coming up made me think of Alex sitting at the window in the hospital.

Friday, April 7, 1944

I keep thinking about Alex up at the hospital. It's not a very nice place for him. I think they should send him home so we can take care of him. I guess I'll go see him tomorrow.

Saturday, April 8, 1944

I went to the hospital today and saw Alex. It still scares me and, I think, probably always will. Alex was sitting in the sunroom again. A nurse told me I could take Alex outside in a wheelchair. I sat in a wooden lawn chair beside him. It was a beautiful day, but I don't think Alex noticed. He said hello to me, but nothing else. I didn't know what to say, so we just sat not talking until it was time for me to go home.

Sunday, April 9, 1944

Sunday school and church. Dad is very mad at Brian, because he is not coming home directly from cadets and keeps missing supper. Brian won't say where he's been. When he gets home he goes to his bedroom and shuts the door. I hate supper at our house these days.

If Brian is home, he and Dad fight all the time. If Brian isn't home, Dad just sits and simmers. Stephen is no good. He pushes his food around his plate and has become what Mother calls a fussy eater and that is making Mother mad. Mother is mad anyway because she can't find her small roasting pan.

"Maybe I lent it to Lily," she said.

Monday, April 10, 1944

I joined the knitting club again today. Everyone made a fuss over my coming back, which is silly, but made me feel good anyway. Nancy runs the club now. I was very surprised that Lydia was there—without Betty! She said her mother made her come. She's actually quite nice to speak to. I never really talked to her much, she was just Betty's other best friend. Thinking about it now, it was hard work being Betty's best friend. I wonder if you grow out of people like you do clothes.

Nancy said she had a very nice pattern for a knitted baby jacket, if I would like to borrow it to make for Caroline's baby.

"I can only do scarves," I told her.

"It's not a hard pattern. I can help you with it. You'll do fine."

I didn't have any knitting started for today, so while the girls knitted I read Dorothy Dix's column to them. It was all about marriage. Dorothy Dix says a woman's marriage is more important to her than a man's is to him. She says a woman's happiness depends upon how successful a man her husband is, and whether her husband is a grouch or a ray of sunshine. She says a woman loses her independence once married and can't go out without asking, whereas a man just goes when he wants.

Nancy said, "Makes you wonder why marriage is so popular. I'm going to become a nun."

"But you're not Catholic," I told her.

Tuesday, April 11, 1944

When I got home there was a note from Mother telling me to go to the corner store, because she heard they were bringing in laundry soap this afternoon. It's been very hard to get laundry soap. I went and stood in a line and about 4:30 the laundry soap got delivered, and the women all ran to grab it and knocked me over. When I finally got to my feet the soap was all gone. So I never did get any, which didn't make Mother very happy.

> *I should go on leave. When they are going to lift the ban is a question we ask ourselves. They will just have to else the fellows go away on their own.*

Wednesday, April 12, 1944

Nancy said, "Dad gave Brian a lift home from the hospital Monday night. He was visiting your brother. It's good for Alex to see all of you." I didn't know Brian went to the hospital after cadets. Why on earth doesn't he tell Dad so they quit fighting?

Mother was sewing a huge stack of flannel into diapers when I got home from school. "You can continue hemming these while I start supper," she said. "Some are for Caroline and the rest are for bombed-out children in Britain."

Sewing isn't my favourite thing, but at least there were no sleeves and neck holes.

Thursday, April 13, 1944

I asked Brian why he didn't tell Dad about visiting Alex on Mondays.

"Who told you that? You just keep your nose out of my business!" he yelled and stamped away to his bedroom.

Our whole house is mad these days. Mother can't find her saucepan.

Friday, April 14, 1944

In science class today we had a bomb drill. I don't know why. At the beginning of the war we were all scared the Germans would come here and bomb us, so we had a lot of drills. But they never came. Last year we had a mock air raid in the city and people pretended to be hurt and all the lights were turned off and the emergency people practised taking care of things. I don't think the Germans ever will come, so I see no need for a bomb drill. Just to show I thought the drill stupid I refused to stick my head totally beneath my desk. Mr. Smith poked it back in with a ruler.

Saturday, April 15, 1944

I had to baby-sit Stephen while Mother and Dad visited Alex, so I took him to Aunt Lily's to work on the garden with me. I told him to bring his planes so he'd have something to do, but he said, "I don't play with them any more." Thinking about it, I haven't seen his planes around lately.

Stephen raked the garden while I did more planning. The newspaper said that to make the best Victory gardens, plant alyssum, lobelia and bellis as an outside border and put vegetables in the middle. I haven't been going to the movies much lately, so I have a bit of baby-sitting money saved up to buy seeds. I know I should be putting it toward Victory Bonds but, in my opinion, a Victory garden is just as patriotic.

Sunday, April 16, 1944

Sunday school and church. I played Scrabble with Stephen. Can any day be more boring than Sunday?

Monday, April 17, 1944

Brian was late home from cadets again. Dad yelled at him so much, I almost started to tell him where Brian had been, but Brian glared at me so fiercely I didn't say anything.

I was just looking out the window right now, and Stephen ran from around back of the garage, looking very suspicious. I wonder what he's up to? Tomorrow is my birthday.

> *On Sunday next it will be my birthday and I will spend it as per usual—just another day.*

Tuesday, April 18, 1944
Morning

Today is my birthday. I am fourteen years old. I don't feel any different. Maybe I'll feel older by the end of the day.

Evening

I had my birthday supper. Everyone came, Aunt Lily and Grandma and even Caroline. Mother and Dad gave me a new purse, much more grown-up looking than any other I've ever got. Brian gave me a new fountain pen. "You must have gone through a million of them," he said. "Always scribbling in your diary. You writing about me?" I must remember to lock up my diary every day.

Stephen gave me a package of lettuce seeds. Aunt Lily gave me two lovely pairs of silky underpants. One blue and one pink. Where she got them I don't know, because silk is hard to come by, but I love them. I have never had such glamorous-looking underwear in my life. "Those will never keep her backside warm," Grandma said. "Good thick cotton or wool would have suited better."

I saw Mother frowning, so I quickly stuck the underpants back in the box, because I was afraid she'd take them to keep "until I was older."

Caroline gave me a gold brooch shaped in the initial *R*. Grandma gave me a Bible with my name written in the front, *Roberta Claire Harrison*.

"Read from it every day," she said sternly. "It'll make you a better person." I already thought I was a pretty good person, except, of course, when I fib.

Mother gave me the last present and said, "This is from Alex." It was a pair of white gloves, but I know it wasn't really from Alex. It's not even something he'd buy me.

Mother made me a cake in the shape of a butterfly with pink icing and fourteen candles on top, except she was quite exasperated because she couldn't find her square cake pan. With everyone there, it almost seemed the same as last year's birthday. Almost.

Wednesday, April 19, 1944

At recess today Betty came over and said, "That must be a new purse. It's very nice."

It was the first she spoke to me since Christmas. I said, "Thank you. I got it for my birthday yesterday."

"Oh," she said. She looked a bit embarrassed. I guess because she used to come for my birthday supper every year. "Have you been to the movies lately?"

"Not a whole lot," I said.

"Maybe we can go some time," she said.

I think Betty wants to be best friends again.

Thursday, April 20, 1944

I went straight to the hospital from school with Nancy and her dad. I don't know why Nancy goes there when she doesn't even have to. My heart still pounds every time I go. Today it was raining so hard we had to sit in the sunroom. There were lots of men in there, but I never look at them. I did once and the man I looked at had the whole side of his face wrinkled from burning. I almost got sick. I don't look anywhere now. I read a book and Alex looks out the window. I'll never get used to him being this way.

I watched Nancy a bit. She laughs and talks to everyone. She reads stories and magazines to them, and gets them drinks. She even talks to the man with the wrinkled face.

I suppose you have all been listening to the news on the radio and probably know more about what is going on than I do.

Friday, April 21, 1944

I finally told Mother my bra pinches. "My goodness," she said. "You certainly have filled out. You must take after your father's side of the family. Heavens knows, it's not ours. We'll get you a new one tomorrow."

I looked at Dad at supper, but it's hard to tell from looking at him whether it's from his side or not that I need a bigger bra.

Saturday, April 22, 1944

Betty called to see if I wanted to go to the movies, but I told her I was going shopping with Mother.

"Are you friends with Betty again?" Mother said.

"I don't know," I told her.

We had to run to catch the bus, and I thought Mother had forgotten our conversation, but once inside she said, "Whatever happened that broke you up with Betty?"

I shrugged. I couldn't very well tell her it was all Caroline's fault, except I know it isn't Caroline's fault really. I think it's Betty's.

We got my new bra at Smallman and Ingram's. It was embarrassing. Mother insisted I try it on right in the store. I've never been naked in a store before! It didn't feel decent. The sales lady wanted to make sure it fit, but I wouldn't let her in the change room. Mother said I make such a fuss over nothing.

On the way out we passed some yellow baby wool that reminded me of spring sunshine.

"Can I have some of that?" I asked Mother.

"Whatever for?" she said.

"Nancy said she'd lend me a pattern to make a sweater for Caroline's baby."

Mother bought me three balls, enough to make matching booties and a hat.

Sunday, April 23, 1944

What an exciting day! I went to Nancy's house. Mother gave me permission, because I was going to start Caroline's baby sweater. I had to take Stephen with me, though, because Mother and Dad were going to the hospital. It didn't matter because Nancy has so many brothers and sisters, one more kid there makes no difference.

Anyway, we were up in Nancy's room when suddenly we heard a lot of commotion downstairs, and it was Nancy's mother having her baby! Rev. Goddard ran all over the house gathering things up and putting them back down again.

"You'd think after eight children he'd be used to this," Nancy said. She got her mother's bag and made sure everything was in it, ready for the hospital. Mrs. Reverend Goddard was very white. She clutched her stomach and moaned, then let out a long breath.

"Do you think your mother would let you stay a bit, Bobby?" she asked me. "Nancy could do with the help to give the children their supper."

I phoned Aunt Lily because Mother wasn't home, and she said certainly I was to stay.

There was a Victory Loan parade downtown in front of the armoury that Brian was marching in with the cadets. So Nancy and I took all the Goddard kids and Stephen, even though it rained. I was surprised to see Brian could move his feet and his arms all at the same time and not get them mixed up. I have $1.25 saved up for war bond stamps. I would have had more but I bought my seeds.

Nancy just phoned me to say she has a new baby brother. I got four rows done on the back of Caroline's baby sweater.

Monday, April 24, 1944

Nancy wasn't at the knitting club but we held it anyway. I started making a pair of socks. Raining all day.

> *…the dust has changed to a sticky, slimy clay mud mire.*

Tuesday, April 25, 1944

It seems like it has been raining for days now.

Wednesday, April 26, 1944

It was as hot as a summer day today and the rain finally stopped. The pavement was steaming and made my blouse and skirt feel wringing wet. Stephen and I went to dig in Aunt Lily's garden. It was fairly water-logged but we didn't care. We just felt like digging around in the dirt. I was greatly tempted to put my seeds in because it was so warm, but I know the rule is don't plant until after May 24th in case of a late frost. Everything has rules, even gardening has rules. I did replant the rose bushes that Aunt Lily hadn't pulled out. I didn't think that would matter, because they were in the ground to start with, so a late frost won't hurt them. Caroline came out while we were there and sat in a chair watching. She looks huge. Just like someone had blown up a balloon inside her blouse. She looked very forlorn sitting there all by herself. I suddenly remembered her dressing up for her dances. She doesn't even wear lipstick now.

The German dead and vehicles strew the roads and fields and stink to the high heavens.

Thursday, April 27, 1944

I went to the hospital to see Alex. Rev. Goddard gave me a ride even though Nancy wasn't going. It was raining again so Alex and I sat in the sunroom. I was reading to him when a man came over.

"Do you know where that girl Nancy is?" he asked.

I spoke at him from behind my book because I didn't want to know if his face was wrinkled. "Her mother had a baby so she is helping out at home."

"Oh, I was hoping she'd write a letter for me," he said.

He sat down in the chair across from Alex and me. I saw him cross his legs from beneath my book and felt quite relieved he had both of them. I kept my face in my book, hoping he'd go away and write his own letter.

Alex got up and went to the washroom.

"I've seen others go like him," the man said suddenly.

Without meaning to I looked up. He had no wrinkles. He didn't look as old as Brian. "Like Alex? Do they get better?" I asked.

He shrugged. "Some do, some don't."

That made me very scared, thinking Alex would never get better.

"What causes it?" I asked. Mother never told me. She and Dad didn't seem to like talking about Alex.

"Seeing something so awful the mind can't handle it. Like maybe seeing your chum's head blown off. The mind blocks something like that right out. Keeps you numb so you don't remember. Oh, sorry, didn't mean to upset you," he said.

He must have seen that I felt a bit woozy thinking of someone's head blown off.

"He saw my Uncle Billy get killed," I told him, though I don't know why I did. I really wanted him just to go.

"That'll do it." The man pulled a package of cigarettes from his dressing gown pocket, knocked it against his knee and shook out two, and left them dangling from his lips. He pulled out a box of matches and opened the box, and with a flick of his wrist a tiny flare shot up and he lit both cigarettes. I couldn't quite see how he did it, though I thought it an awfully awkward way to light a cigarette.

Alex came back and sat down.

"Want a smoke?" the man asked him.

Alex didn't answer, but the man leaned over and held one out to him. As he bent I saw his bathrobe sleeve swing free, no arm inside it. Even now, writing about that sleeve hanging empty makes my stomach quiver.

Friday, April 28, 1944

I saw Betty laughing and carrying on with Rick Anderson and, strangely, I didn't even care. I tried to, but I couldn't. Mother says this is getting ridiculous—now her wash basin is gone!

We're not sleeping in any luxurious beds of satin, but
they tell us our slit trenches are much safer.

Saturday, April 29, 1944

I might be pretty, and let me be crystal clear on this, I didn't say it myself so I'm not being immodest.

Here is how it happened:

I went to the hospital to see Alex today. The man with the empty sleeve came to sit with us. He gave Alex a cigarette again. It's funny how Alex will eat and smoke and walk, and he'll say hello when I get there, but he won't say anything else.

Anyway, I didn't know where to look because I didn't want the man catching me staring at his sleeve, though that's all I seemed to see. Today it was pinned up to his shoulder so it was out of the way.

"Do you know when Nancy will be back?" he asked. "I really want to write my folks and let them know how I'm doing. I'm practising writing with my left hand, but my letters look like a chicken walked across the page."

"I don't think it will be for a while," I said. "Her mother needs her at home. I guess I could write your letter," I said and immediately wished I hadn't offered. I only wanted that empty sleeve to go away. I don't want to think about what's under there. But when I said that, his face lit up.

"That would be swell!" he said. "I'll be right back with paper and a pen."

The whole time he was gone I thought maybe I should sneak out of the hospital, but he came back too fast and handed me the paper and pen, then settled himself back on the chair.

"Right-o then," he said. "Just write what I say."

I picked up the pen, waiting.

"Dear Mother and Father," he began. "I'm having this letter written by the prettiest girl in London."

I was so embarrassed. I hoped no one else in the room heard him. I stole a look at Alex, but he didn't seem to hear.

"I can't write that," I told the man.

"Why not?" he said. "Besides, it's my letter, so you have to write what I say."

So I wrote it.

His name is George, by the way, and he's from a little town in Saskatchewan. He has two brothers over at the war and one sister at home. George has blonde hair, pale blue eyes and a long, narrow face. His smile is sort of lopsided. He's actually very homely, except he's not.

I've been thinking about what George said about Alex seeing something so awful his mind went numb. Alex has to be helped soon or he might not get better. I can't imagine him never being better. I have to figure out a way to make Alex like he used to be.

I just looked at myself in the mirror. I'm passable, but I'm certainly not pretty. George must have been fibbing.

Sunday, April 30, 1944

It is a beautiful day. Too beautiful to be sitting in church. I visited with Nancy in the afternoon so she could help me with Caroline's baby sweater. I took Stephen with me. He comes home with a bit of colour in his face when he plays with the Goddard kids, which I am glad to see, because he's sneaking around the backyard a lot lately and I'm worried about him. Mother doesn't seem to mind my going out on Sundays any more. But then everything seems to have changed.

I asked Nancy about George. She said he's eighteen. He'd lied about his age and joined the army when he was sixteen. He drove a tank in the war. She didn't know how he'd lost his arm. "I'll listen if they tell me, but I won't ask," she said. "And George never told me."

Many of us were split up and I'm wondering where I'm going to be placed. It is too bad. I hated to leave many of them for they were all the finest fellows.

Monday, May 1, 1944

May Day. My sock actually looks like a real sock. I'm not such a bad knitter after all. If only Mrs. Ford was here to see it.

Tuesday, May 2, 1944

I couldn't wait. It was such a warm day today and we have not had any cold weather lately, so I planted my radish, green onion and lettuce seeds. Stephen and I had made little furrows in the dirt last week, so all we had to do was drop them in and cover them up. At first I didn't want Stephen helping, because it was my garden, but he's very good company even if he doesn't talk much, and he likes mucking around in dirt like I do.

Grandma and Aunt Lily came to supper tonight. Caroline was going to come but she was not feeling well.

"Planting seeds early just invites a frost," Grandma told me.

I noticed weeds don't seem to get hurt by frost.

Wednesday, May 3, 1944

Dad was listening to the radio tonight and said the war seemed to be going better, except on May 1st the Athabaska warship was sunk. Mother said as far as she was concerned it all ended for her when Alex came home. "Though it will not end for Mrs. Goddard until her boy returns. And if he never comes home, it'll never end for her," Mother added.

Canadian bomber squadrons fly missions every night now and Dad never misses a news report. Even though he doesn't say anything, I know he's thinking about James.

How the cities on the continent can stand the big bombing raids is a question, for the RAF are systematically destroying cities, factories and everything of importance used to fight and make war supplies.

Thursday, May 4, 1944

I went to the hospital today to see Alex. George was playing cards but when he saw me he came over right away. We pushed Alex outside in a wheelchair. George said Alex has been getting his leg exercised regularly and he should be walking soon.

We walked over to a baseball diamond. George said he'd been practising his batting and wasn't too bad for a one-armed fellow. He said that he had to stay at the hospital until his stump healed. It was being very stubborn. I had almost forgotten about his arm being gone until he said that. What an awfully ugly word—stump.

Friday, May 5, 1944

Betty asked me to her house after school today. I was so surprised I didn't know what to say so I said yes.

Her mother said, "Why Roberta, how lovely to see you. It has been such a long time since you've been here."

I felt embarrassed, though I don't know what I had to be embarrassed about, but I started babbling, "I've been very busy. I've been putting in my aunt's Victory garden and I've been visiting my brother at the veteran's hospital."

"Oh, dear," she said. "I don't think the hospital with all those men is a very nice place for a young girl like you to be."

"I don't think it's a very nice place for anyone to be, especially those soldiers," I said. She raised her eyebrows and I realized I probably sounded impertinent.

Betty showed me her graduation dress she and her mother made a special trip to Toronto to buy. In six weeks we are out of school and we are having a graduation dance. I hadn't thought much about my dress until now. It was the first time in a long time I'd felt the Worm of Jealousy twist, but it did when I saw how beautiful Betty's dress was, just not as much as before. Strangely though, I always thought Betty's house lovely and quiet, but now I think it's more like a lonely quiet. I must be more used to Nancy's noisy house now.

Brian was in another parade, so we all went and saw him march down Dundas Street. There are so many parades all the time. Sometimes I try to remember what it was like before the war was on, but I have a hard time. It seems to me the streets have always been full of uniforms. I thought Brian looked quite nice marching with all the others in his uniform. I even told him that.

Saturday, May 6, 1944

I can't believe that in six weeks we will be out of school, and I will be in high school next September. Brian says, "Enjoy being the King of the Hill now, because next year you'll be at the bottom again." He always tries to ruin everything.

Mother has borrowed a nice pattern for my graduation dress from a lady at the workshop. It's a princess-style dress with the waist cut high, which Mother assures me is quite elegant. She showed me some material she picked up on sale, though it was still quite expensive. It is a soft yellow, the same colour as the baby wool I bought. I can't believe she is making me a whole new dress!

I told Alex and George at the hospital all about the dance. I decided I am going to talk to Alex just like he was listening and talking back to me, even if he doesn't. I asked George what he thought about that idea, and he thought it a very good one.

George said he wished he'd finished high school instead of running off to war. He said it seemed like quite an adventure at the time, but it didn't turn out to be at all what he expected. He said he might go back to school now. The government would pay him to do so because he's a returning soldier, and he wouldn't be much use as a farm worker with just one arm.

Mother made us pull the entire basement apart because she is missing more pots. We never found them.

Sunday, May 7, 1944

Dad planted his garden after church.

"I decided I wanted to invite that frost your Grandma was going on about," he said. "Besides, we'll be eating lettuce and green onions while she's still dropping seeds on the 24th."

Monday, May 8, 1944

Today is Brian's sixteenth birthday, but it wasn't a very good one. He came home late again so we ate his birthday supper without him. Mother cried. Dad started yelling as soon as the door opened, so Brian turned around and walked right back out.

I've seen columns of German prisoners on their way to the cages. The Germans are a depleted and haggard lot, some only youths of 15 and 18, not even shaving yet.

Tuesday, May 9, 1944

When I got to the hospital, George had put Alex at the table where the men were playing cards.

"I decided your idea to treat him like normal was a good one," he said. "So I've been sitting him down here with us. Some of the fellows weren't too keen at first, but then one said he had a really good poker face, and after that they didn't mind."

I told Alex and George more about the pattern for my graduation dress and how it was coming along. Then all of a sudden, I realized George was smoking and staring out the window, so I apologized for talking so much. "I'm sorry," I said. "I didn't mean to go on so long about my dress."

George looked very surprised. "No," he said. "I was just thinking how sick I am of this place, and how nice it would be to do something normal like go to a dance. Just get up and go to a dance. I've done nothing normal in almost two years. That's the problem with this place. It's not normal. It's like there's a whole world out there and we're not part of it. We're stuck here isolated." He nodded towards Alex and looked quite disgusted.

Then he said, "I think yellow would suit your hair very well."

Wednesday, May 10, 1944

I saw Nancy's baby brother today. I've never seen anything so tiny, yet so perfect. I can't believe I was once that small.

"Wouldn't Brent love to see him?" Mrs. Goddard said. After Mrs. Goddard took the baby upstairs to nurse I asked Nancy, "Do they let Brent write you?" I'd never asked her before. Afraid I guess, though that's just plain silly.

"Yes. He writes that he's fine," Nancy said. "But I doubt he is. Brent liked to fly because he loved wide, open spaces. How he must hate being locked up."

Then she told me all about Brent. I should have asked Nancy about her brother before. I see that now. I am so stupid at times.

After I left Nancy's I went to Aunt Lily's and checked the garden. There are little green shoots where I planted lettuce and onions. I walked down one row as far as the fence, and I saw there were little green shoots coming up there, too, where the love-lies-bleeding had been. Maybe Stephen accidentally put radish seeds in there. I'll have to ask him.

Thursday, May 11, 1944

I told Stephen he had to go by himself to our garden and take out some of the weeds, because I had to go to the hospital. He looked very proud when I called it our garden. At the hospital, George was trying to take the lid off his fountain pen to show me how well he could write with his left hand, except it wouldn't come off, so I suddenly grabbed it. "Let me," I said and pulled the lid from the pen.

He stood up so fast his chair banged over making me jump. His face was very red. "Don't ever do that again!" he yelled at me, but I didn't notice him because I realized that Alex was trembling all over. His hand was shaking on the chair arm. George immediately leaned over and put his arm around Alex's shoulder and said, "It's all right, old man. Didn't mean to scare you."

George continued rubbing Alex's shoulder and I suddenly remembered the pictures Alex sent where the soldiers always had their arms around each other, and I suddenly knew why. That was all they had over there at the war—each other.

This morning a horse came across the field. No one owned it. The poor animal just strolled around aimlessly. I could see it looked lost, no one cared about it and it went on its way.

Friday, May 12, 1944

I think I have a plan to make Alex better, but I'm not writing it down in case I jinx it.

Saturday, May 13, 1944

Felt sick with my period so I lay down most of the day and didn't go to see Alex. I was surprised I missed not going.

Later in the evening, I felt better so went and saw Caroline. She told me you don't get your period when you're expecting. "One of the few bonuses," she said. "One of the very few."

I asked Caroline if she was happy being married. "How should I know?" she said. "I was only married a couple of weeks and James went away."

I told her Dorothy Dix says that illogical as it is, women on the whole were happier married than single even when their marriages were not very successful. She says they are better off even if they are worse off.

"Why do you even read that stuff?" Caroline asked.

Hers was the only remaining house left on the street
and even it had the windows smashed.

Sunday, May 14, 1944

Today is Mother's Day. Smallman and Ingram's ran a huge full-page ad in the newspaper yesterday saying *Mother Bravest Soldier of All.*

George telephoned me from the hospital while we were having lunch. Mother looked very surprised to hear a man's voice ask for me.

"Your brother had a really bad nightmare last night," he told me.

"Oh no!" I said.

"No. No. It's a good thing. It means he's starting to remember, and he needs to remember in order to get better."

When I got off the phone Mother asked me who that was.

"It's a friend of Alex's from the hospital," I told her. "He said Alex needs cigarettes." I crossed my fingers behind my back, though I knew it was still a fib. I wonder how crossing fingers actually gets rid of a fib, but everyone I know seems to think it does.

She looked at me quite hard. "Funny he would call to tell you that. I'll take some up when I go today."

One of my chums here had a big parcel come to him
from Canada the other day and we both had a rare
treat from it. He shared with me some real Canadian
cheese, sausages, jam and fruit.

Monday, May 15, 1944

Nancy is back at knitting club. We have a lot more girls in our club now, most of the Grade Eights in fact. I finished my pair of socks, but I didn't put them in the bag with the others. I waited until everyone was gone and asked Nancy if she thought them good enough for her brother in the prisoner-of-war camp.

She looked at them a long time, then said, "They're absolutely perfect. Thank you, Bobby. I'll send them with the next package."

Tuesday, May 16, 1944

Mother went to get out her big preserving kettle to dye some clothes but it was gone. I think there is a thief at work here.

Wednesday, May 17, 1944

Mother had a long talk with me after school and told me how babies are made. She was so uncomfortable I wanted to tell her I knew, but then that might be telling on Nancy, so I just sat and nodded my head. She said I couldn't date until I was sixteen. I think it was George calling me that made her tell me about babies. And Caroline too.

> *Never in all my experience and in my eyes will I*
> *forget the tremendous sight of the air armadas. The*
> *sky is thick with more planes than birds. Their noise*
> *never ceases day or night.*

Thursday, May 18, 1944

George and I took Alex for a long walk through the hospital grounds. George's face looked grey and there were purple circles under his eyes. We had to stop and sit down a couple of times so he could rest. I think he's sick, but when I asked him, he waved his hand and said, "I'm fine, just didn't sleep well last night."

While we were out a plane went overhead and Alex cringed. George put his hand on Alex's shoulder until the plane went away. "Normally you wouldn't notice a single plane, but it's so quiet here," George said. "It was the first thing I thought when we got to London. It's so quiet. War's so noisy."

Friday, May 19, 1944

At school today Nancy told me George had to have an emergency operation last night because he has gangrene in his arm. They phoned her father to come out, because for a little while it looked like George might not pull through. I couldn't think at all at school today. I shouldn't have made him walk yesterday. I probably made him sicker.

Saturday, May 20, 1994

It's a holiday weekend, but I don't feel much like holidaying. I'm very worried about George. Then I got mad that I had to worry. I'm tired of people being sick all the time. I'm tired of worrying about George and Alex and Brian being miserable and Stephen being too quiet and Dad not talking to Caroline. I want them all to go away and leave me alone. I pulled up weeds so hard in the garden this afternoon that Stephen asked "Are you mad at them?"

I had to laugh and things seemed a bit better then.

The leaves over by the fence don't look like anything else in the garden. Also, they are in the exact place I tore out the love-lies-bleeding, but that couldn't be. I looked it up in Dad's gardening encyclopedia and it says they are an annual plant.

Sunday, May 21, 1944

Church and Sunday school. I told Mother I was going over to

111

Nancy's for the afternoon and I took Stephen with me. It was a bit of a fib, though I really did go to Nancy's, so it wasn't a real fib. I wonder if you fib on Sunday if that is worse than the rest of the week. What about on Sunday at the minister's house! The only worse place would be in church.

I left Stephen playing with Nancy's brothers and sisters. Their house is so happy, and I noticed Stephen grinning on the way over just thinking about going.

Anyway, Nancy and I went to the hospital with Nancy's dad. We found George's ward, and Nancy stood guard while I sneaked in to see him because we weren't supposed to be in the wards.

The dormitory was very long and there were lots of white metal beds, though most didn't have men in them. Finally I found George at the very end. He looked very thin lying under the white sheet. The room was hot and smelled horrible even though some windows were open. George wasn't moving and at first I thought he might be dead, then he turned his head and saw me and said, "Bobby. What are you doing here?"

"Are you going to get better?" I asked. I could feel sweat trickle down my back and the walls began to swim around me, but I gritted my teeth and hung on to the end of his bed.

"Sure," he said, and tried to smile, but his smile was more lop-sided than usual. He doesn't look as old as Stephen, I thought to myself, and I suddenly realized he could die. He could really die. And his mother and dad are in Saskatchewan.

"You've got to get better because I want you to come to my graduation dance," I blurted out. The room was whirling around so fast I could hardly stand upright. "But I can't date until I'm sixteen so we'll have to go as friends," I babbled.

"I'd like that," he said. "I promise I'll be better by then." His smile got bigger, then suddenly he went to sleep.

I staggered out to the hall where Nancy was and fainted dead away. When I woke up I was in the broom closet. Nancy said she'd seen Mother and Dad coming down the hall to visit Alex and had dragged me in there so they wouldn't see me. In movies the heroine always faints gracefully away into the hero's arms, and then he lays her lovingly onto a handy couch. He never drags her by the feet into a broom closet.

It's very noisy here and the only time I feel like
sleeping is when it's time to get up.

Monday, May 22, 1944

A holiday from school. My graduation dance is in one month. I can't believe I actually asked George to the dance. Mother will have a fit. We started my dress today, checking everything twice before we began cutting because the material was so dear and we didn't want to ruin it. Finally, Mother started sewing the darts, and I heard her muttering some words she gets mad at Brian for saying. She saw me looking at her and said, "This slippery material is a beggar to work on."

Tuesday, May 23, 1944

George isn't really that much older than me. He's eighteen and I'm fourteen. That's only four years difference and, after all, Dad is nine years older than mother. I wonder what Dorothy Dix would say. I wonder what Mother is going to say.

Wednesday, May 24, 1944

It's very hard to sit still in school these days. The warm breeze floats flower smells through the windows, birds sing, yet I have to pay attention because if I don't pass my final exams I won't graduate. The only one I'm really worried about is Math. I couldn't imagine staying in this school another year! I went by Aunt Lily's on the way home from school. Caroline came out with me to look at the garden. She waddles when she walks now.

I pulled up a radish, but it was very tiny, so I put it back in the dirt. I hope it grows bigger but I might have killed it.

"What is that coming up near the fence?" Caroline asked.

"I think it's honeysuckle," I told her, even though I never planted honeysuckle. I really hope it's not love-lies-bleeding. If so, I'll have to pull it out before Aunt Lily sees it.

We often have a cheap lighting system when an enemy flare lights near us. It lights everything up and you can read or thread a needle it's so bright.

Thursday, May 25, 1944

I went to the hospital today. I couldn't get past the nurse to see George as he's still in bed. I was just as glad because I feel really embarrassed that I asked him to the dance. Let's face it, he wouldn't want to go to a kids' dance. He was just being nice.

I put my plan to make Alex better into action today. I remember how Alex used to love words, and I hoped he might still like them. I brought my diary and I'm reading to him from it about the time when he was at the war. It was cool outside, so I picked the far end of the sunroom because I didn't want everybody to hear. I read the part about the Worm of Jealousy and the knitting club. I pointed out to him the words I had been keeping for him, though I don't do that any more. Maybe I should. I think he's listening because he sat quieter than usual. It's probably a dumb idea but I can't think of any other.

While I was reading, Nancy brought George into the sunroom in a wheelchair.

"I sneaked him past the nurse," she said.

George looked pale and tired, but he was smiling. I couldn't believe how happy I was to see him. That worries me.

Friday, May 26, 1944

Aunt Lily came to the house this evening and she was all dressed up. I told her she looked like a movie star or a model and she told me not to be so silly, but blushed.

"Are you going out somewhere?" I asked.

Her eyes jumped around the room, looking everywhere but at me. "Just out, nowhere special," she said. "Is your mother around?"

I called Mother up from the basement where she was getting a jar of pickles. She came into the kitchen and took one look at Aunt Lily and her eyebrows went straight up into her hair.

"It's nearly six months now and I hadn't seen Billy for close to two years before that," Aunt Lily said, even though Mother hadn't said a word.

Mother thumped the pickles on the counter.

"Well, I'm not a bloody nun!" Aunt Lily hissed. I think she forgot I was there.

Mother's shoulders slumped down. "I know," she said. Then she and Aunt Lily hugged. They were smiling, yet tears ran down their faces.

"It's just a dance," Aunt Lily sobbed. "And he's really very nice. Just don't tell Mother."

She sounded just like me right then.

This isn't exactly a picnic…

Saturday, May 27, 1944

Alex was sleeping when I went to the hospital today. George said he'd heard Alex had a rough night. I don't know if that is good or not. Nancy asked if I would help her serve ginger ale to the men who couldn't get to the canteen. I couldn't think of any way to refuse, though I really didn't want to help. I had a tray of full glasses and suddenly realized that the man with the burnt face was on my side of the room and George was talking to him. I didn't know what to do. I quickly looked around for Nancy, but she wasn't anywhere to be seen.

I couldn't *not* give the man his pop, because he'd know why. My legs wobbled all the way over and my palms were so sweaty I thought I'd drop the tray, so I put it down and picked up two glasses. I handed one to George and handed the other quickly to the burnt man without looking at him and started to go away when George said, "Bobby, Larry here is a bona fide war hero. They're bringing up a special surgeon from the States just to give him back his pretty face."

I realized it would be rude to leave, so I took a deep breath and turned and looked straight at his burnt face, and said, "Hello." Then I turned to George. "I guess there's nothing they can do about your face. Guess you're just stuck with it."

I couldn't believe I said that. But Larry started laughing and George slapped his knee and joined him.

"You have a brother, Brian, right? He comes and talks to me all the time when he's visiting Alex," Larry said.

I was very surprised to hear that.

It turns out Larry landed a plane that was in flames rather than

116

bail out, because his gunners couldn't get out and he didn't want the plane to go down with them in it. He saved them but got badly burned. He's actually very nice and I really hope they make his face better.

Nancy and I went to the show this evening. Mother says since I am spending Saturday afternoon with Alex, it's only right I still get to go to the show, even if it's at night. We saw Susan Hayward and John Wayne in *The Fighting Seabees*, U.S. Navy supermen. They should do a movie about Canadian supermen like Larry.

Sunday, May 28, 1944

Mother wasn't feeling very well today so she decided to stay home from church. Dad said he thought he'd better stay home, too.

"You're perfectly healthy," Mother said to Dad. "There's no reason for you to miss church."

"I wouldn't go anywhere without you, my dear," Dad said.

"You'll take any excuse to stay home from church," Mother said.

I said, "Maybe I won't go to Sunday school either. I could get you some tea."

"You're going," Mother said. "And I'll expect to hear from you and Brian what the sermon was about."

On the way home from church I told Brian I'd met Larry.

Brian glanced nervously at me, then stared at his feet. "Larry's a swell fellow," was all he said.

Caroline's baby sweater is nearly done. I just have to sew the sleeves together and put on buttons. It is so tiny it'd fit a doll.

I was looking for Stephen this afternoon to go to the garden and went into his room and noticed his planes are all missing from his dresser. When I found him, he was coming in from the backyard and looking just like me when I'm doing something I shouldn't be.

Monday, May 29, 1944

I tried to tell Mother about George going to the dance with me, but she banged cupboards open and closed looking for her strainer. I thought it best not to *incur* her *wrath* right now. I decided to collect words for Alex again.

*We all wish the war was over so we could go home
and begin where we left off.*

Tuesday, May 30, 1944

Some of the girls stand at the back fence talking to Betty at recess, but most of us bring our knitting outside and sit on the steps and talk and knit. We decided we want to have all our socks, mitts and scarves done before the end of school.

Wednesday, May 31, 1944

Nancy asked me if I was in love with George and if that was why I invited him to the dance.

"Don't be so silly," I told her. "We're just going as friends."

I felt so odd after talking to Nancy about George. My stomach felt sick and my eyes kept tearing up. Either I'm getting my period or I really am in love with George.

*There are mass burying places where many are put
who were killed. Also some who are not identified
but their relatives come and place flowers not knowing which grave they are in but still knowing they lie
somewhere.*

Thursday, June 1, 1944

I asked George if he thought Alex was getting better. It seems some days he is, but some days he's not. Today was a "not" day. Alex totally ignored George and me. George said it was just a slight setback, but once Alex gets going, his recovery will be quick. It takes a long while to get over the memories of war.

"What was it like in Italy?" I asked.

"Bloody hell," George said. "And I'm not swearing just to hear it. You know I'm not a swearing man. It was bloody hell."

He was quiet a long time. "When I first joined the army I thought it exciting crossing the ocean, seeing new places besides the farm and getting a regular pay cheque, too. Ended up we sat around England a long time and that was boring, though I got to see more of the place than a farmer's kid from Saskatchewan probably would ever see.

"I thought the soldiering part would be easy. I've hunted before, knew about rifles and guns. Turned out I was just a farmer's kid. I'm not a soldier. Nor were any of the others over there. I mean, I've seen some bad things on the farm, but nothing like that. Nothing like that," he repeated. "No wonder your brother ended up like he did. And that's not cowardice, you know," George assured me. "I'd rather be side by side with a man who cracked, than one who didn't. No heart to a man if he can stand what we did and not have it bother him. And that's all I'm going to say about it. All I'll ever tell you about it."

Friday, June 2, 1944

I pulled my first leaves of lettuce from the garden. Stephen was supposed to come help me weed, but he was playing with Nancy's brothers. He goes over there by himself now. When I got to Aunt

Lily's I couldn't find Caroline at first. Finally I found her in her room, crying.

"Are you having the baby?" I asked.

"No," she said. "I'm just feeling a bit blue. Mother says this happens when you're expecting, but that doesn't make me feel any better. I want James." I gave her my lettuce leaves to make a fresh salad.

Saturday, June 3, 1944

George and Alex both walked outside today, though we didn't go very far. George is very white, but he looks better. Alex limps, but he's walking better. We watched some men bowling for a bit, mainly because I didn't know what to do about reading my diary, so finally I told George my plan. He thought it a great idea. I stumbled a lot at first because I was embarrassed reading it, though I did skip all the female stuff. I thought that would embarrass them more. Alex actually smiled at something in my diary, and said, "That's Brian for you." George says it's a start.

Before I left the hospital George asked, "Are you sure you really want me to go with you to your graduation dance? I mean, there must be lots of boys in your class wanting to take you."

I nearly fell over my own feet at that. Lots of boys! No one ever asked me out. Except almost that time with Rick Anderson.

Then I thought, maybe he doesn't want to go and is looking for a way to get out of it.

"You don't have to go if you don't want to," I told him.

He looked quite surprised. "Oh, I want to go," he said. "I thought maybe you felt sorry for me being sick and asked me. I thought maybe you wouldn't want me there, with this and all," he gestured to his arm.

"I don't see your arm any more when I look at you," I told him.

And I really meant it.

"I don't see it either," he said. "But that's because it's not there." And he gave me his huge lopsided grin.

Sunday, June 4, 1944

I told Dad that Caroline was feeling very low. I wanted to tell him to go talk to her but I didn't know how, so I said, "Yes, Caroline is quite low," once, then twice, then I said it a third time. He was precariously balanced on one foot on the stepladder, fishing dead leaves out of the gutters at the time.

"Bobby, are you going to stand there all afternoon repeating yourself?" he asked testily. "Make yourself useful. Hold this ladder steady."

Mother says, with a man you have to pick your time carefully to talk to them. I don't think it's just with men. I am still looking for a good time to tell Mother about George and the dance.

Monday, June 5, 1944

Today is our last knitting club day at school, though we voted to meet at each other's houses once a week through the summer. After knitting club, I went to Nancy's house for supper and we practised our dancing. Nancy insisted we try jitterbugging.

"Why?" I asked. "The principal will never let us jitterbug."

"We'll see about that," Nancy said.

We moved her sister's bed into the hall to make more room and practised for an hour until Rev. Goddard called up, "Let's leave the ceilings in one piece. This is church property, you know."

> *It won't be long before this thing is over at the rate Jerry is being chased and this is the kill and I wouldn't miss it for anything.*

Tuesday, June 6, 1944

The newspaper had huge headlines today covering half the front page—INVASION ARMY STABS SEVERAL MILES INLAND.

"This is it," Dad said. "And not a moment too soon. This will be the end of the war."

Still haven't told Mother about George.

Wednesday, June 7, 1944

It's Dad's birthday. I have no idea how old he is because he won't say. But he's old. Had my first green onion and radish from my garden. Grandma came to supper tonight and Dad insisted on putting out my green onion, radish and a few of his lettuce leaves.

"Help yourself to some greens there, Helen," he said to Grandma.

Grandma gave him such a look even Mother couldn't help smiling, and Aunt Lily giggled outright. Caroline was at supper, too. She looked absolutely miserable. I saw Dad looking at her out of the corner of his eye.

According to the paper, D-Day is going very well. At school the teachers were all excited, and we had an assembly to tell us what was happening. Nancy says she hopes it finishes fast so her brother can come home.

Brian is very quiet these days.

Mother is fuming. Her big frying pan is gone!

When I get back will take you for a holiday as I am going to take one myself-where it is good and quiet and away from everybody and everything.

Thursday, June 8, 1944

Drizzly, foggy day, so Alex and I had to sit in the sunroom. Everyone was talking about the end of the war coming soon. George was back in bed with a bit of a fever. While I was reading to Alex (quietly so no one would overhear my diary), a nurse came in. "Your young man wants to see you," she said.

"Who?" I asked.

"Your young man, George Lake," she repeated. "You're not supposed to be in the wards, but I think we can make an exception this time."

"He's not my young man," I mumbled *wretchedly*. "We're just friends." Every eye in that place was on me. Walking to the door, my legs felt like wood. Even Alex watched me.

George had two bright red spots on his cheeks and he moved his legs restlessly beneath the sheets. I was quite alarmed to see him looking like that.

"Just a bit of fever," he said. "The doctors tell me the arm's trying to heal itself. I promise I'll be right as rain for your dance, though. I'm not going to miss the only graduation dance I've been invited to."

Friday, June 9, 1944

I took Dad's gardening encyclopaedia over to Aunt Lily's. The leaves of the plant coming up near the fence match those in the picture. There's no two ways about it—it's love-lies-bleeding all right. I got out the trowel and got down on my knees to dig it out, but I couldn't do it. It's just started to grow. I can't kill it. I love everything that is growing in my garden. I don't know what to tell Aunt Lily. Maybe she'll never notice.

This is not as comfortable a life as I've been used to living in billets, but at night here it's a slit trench, but I can't yet agree it is any worse than the filth of Italy and the smell of rottenness everywhere.

Caroline had her baby today! Here is how it happened:

I went over to weed, and I poked my head in the door and yelled, "It's just me, Caroline."

I heard little whimpering sounds, so I went in and found Caroline lying on the couch.

Her face went rigid and she yelled and clutched her stomach. "Get Mother, Bobby!" she yelled. "I'm having the baby."

I ran back to our house, but I couldn't find anybody there. Then I remembered Aunt Lily and Mother had gone out shopping. I screamed frantically all over the house.

"What the hell's all the noise about?" Dad came storming in from the garage.

"Caroline's having her baby," I gasped.

Dad headed out the door with me pounding close behind. I never knew Dad could run that fast. When Caroline saw Dad she started crying, "Dad. I'm so scared, Dad."

"Nothing to be scared of. I've been through this five times (though I think he meant Mother has), so I know what to do."

Dad got Aunt Lily's car keys and we helped Caroline into the car.

"I'm so sorry, Dad," Caroline kept saying all the way to the hospital.

Dad's mouth got tight, then he pursed his lips and frowned. It was interesting, all the *contortions* his face went through, then he put his hand over Caroline's. "You're not the one who needs to be sorry," he muttered.

I don't know if Caroline heard because she started yelling the baby was coming, though it really wasn't.

I waited in the hospital waiting room for hours. I phoned Mother around suppertime, and she and Aunt Lily came to the hospital and we all waited together. Finally, a nurse came in and told Mother and Dad to come with her.

I got really scared, but they came back right away. "It's a boy," Dad said. "A real beaut."

Caroline had a baby boy. I couldn't see him yet, because the hospital said I was a kid and kids weren't allowed in the wards. I wanted to tell them I went to a hospital two times a week and even gave drinks to people with burned faces. But I didn't.

All the way home Dad kept saying, "My grandson. A real beaut of a grandson." I think Caroline is Dad's favourite again, but I don't mind.

Sunday, June 11, 1944

I went to the hospital today because Mother and Dad were with Caroline. I told Alex he was an uncle. He smiled. We practised walking up and down the corridors today. George was still in bed. Sunday is a real visiting day up at the hospital and there were lots of people around, so Alex and I sneaked into George's ward. I figure we're the closest thing to George's family anyway, and he should have visitors, too. Alex lit a cigarette for George though I don't think they're supposed to be smoking in their rooms.

I read a bit more to them from my diary. I just realized I will not be able to read the parts about George. I'll just have to fib again and say that's all there is. I'm getting very good at fibbing.

Before I left, George said, "Bobby, keep an eye on Brian. He was up here Monday asking me and some of the other guys how we got into the army under age."

Monday, June 12, 1944

Ten days until the dance. I still haven't told Mother.

> *Our general guess over here is we will have to go to
> Japan after it's over here. Well, there is one fellow
> here that thinks he has been enough places now
> without seeing any more of the world.*

Tuesday, June 13, 1944

Mother was still at her workshop and Dad wasn't home from work yet, when Brian came in all excited like he had a big secret.

"What are you looking like that for?" I demanded.

"Like what?"

"Like the cat that got the cream," I told him. Suddenly I remembered what George said.

"You signed up, didn't you?" I shrieked.

Stephen stood on the bottom step watching, eyes wide.

"Don't be stupid," Brian said. He started to go out of the room, but I grabbed his arm.

"You're too young. You'll get hurt like Alex and George and Larry..."

Brian shook my hand off his arm. I heard the back door open, but I was too busy with Brian to notice who came in.

"That's why I did it. Because of them. I've heard their stories."

"Did what? Whose stories?" Dad stood in the kitchen doorway, Mother hovering behind him.

"He goes to the hospital every Monday after cadets and visits the men. He's finding out how he can sign up underage," I told them. I didn't want to tell on Brian, but I didn't want Brian to go to war, either.

"I can help over there. The men at the hospital told me what was going on and how they needed more men, they were so short-handed. I can help," Brian said. "I'm big for my age. I can do anything most men can do." He lifted his chin and stared at Dad. "I'm not scared, you know."

"I know you're not scared," Dad said. "But you're only sixteen."

"I'm already signed up," Brian interrupted.

Mother opened her mouth, but Dad spoke before she could.

"We'll talk about it in the garage."

They came in about an hour later. Brian's eyes were red. I didn't look at him so he'd think I didn't know he'd been crying. Mother looked like she wanted to hug him and smack him both, but we put out their suppers instead.

Wednesday, June 14, 1944

My dress fits perfectly! It has princess lines, with a v back with a bow. Aunt Lily is lending me a necklace.

Thursday, June 15, 1944

Didn't go to the hospital because I had to study for exams starting Monday. I have to pass.

These people have had some hardships by the look of them.

Friday, June 16, 1944

Brian is not signed up any more.

"Every time I saw Alex or talked to those guys," he told me, "I felt like I should go over and take their place. Not be sitting here doing nothing. I was even mad at them because I thought war was all glory, but those guys up there soon spoiled that for me."

"I'd be scared to go to war," I told him.

He looked uncomfortable a moment, then said, "I was. A bit. That's one reason I thought I'd better do it soon so I wouldn't chicken out."

"George told me they were all scared," I said. "I think you're brave."

Saturday, June 17, 1944

I didn't go to the hospital today because I have to study for exams. Nancy came over and we studied Geography and History. We took a little break and read Dorothy Dix's column in the newspaper about how to tell a boy not to put his arm around you in the show. She wrote about how it looks common and goofy to spoon in public, and how boys are trying to show off what wolves they are. Then Nancy began to howl like a wolf until I fell off my bed laughing.

"If a few good hints don't work," she read, "a good jab in the arm with a hat pin will cause any amorous youth to remove his arm promptly."

"But I don't wear a hat," I told Nancy.

"I don't have an amorous youth," Nancy said.

Then we practised our dancing until Mother said, "It doesn't sound like much studying is going on up there."

Sunday, June 18, 1944

Church and Sunday school. I thought I'd studied enough and wanted to go out in the afternoon, but Mother said I had to stay in. I read a book because I didn't think I could stuff any more information into my brain without seriously hurting it.

The dust is choking and the sun dry and hot. Caens,

*which you have heard a lot about, is more of a mess
when actually passing there. There isn't a house left
standing, it is just dust and rubble.*

Monday, June 19, 1944

I wrote Math in the morning and History in the afternoon.

Tuesday, June 20, 1944

I wrote Geography in the morning and had the afternoon off to study Science. Caroline brought home the baby today. She is calling him William—Billy, after Uncle Billy. I gave her the sweater, bonnet and booties I knitted and she said they fit Billy to a *T*.

*There certainly must have been some fierce battles
for everywhere the destruction is terrible.*

ARMED FORCES AIR LETT

Open Here

Summer 1944

Mr & Mrs L Haworth
Bay Ave, Richmond Hill
Ontario, Canada

Wednesday, June 21, 1944

I saw Stephen sneaking out to the backyard with something under his arm, so I followed him. He put what he was carrying in the rain barrel behind the garage. After he left, I looked in and there were Mother's pots and pans and Stephen's planes.

I found Stephen and asked him what he was doing hiding all Mother's pans.

"I'm collecting them for the war effort," he told me. "For the metal drive."

"But you don't have to give them your planes," I said.

"I want to. Do you think Mother will be mad?"

We both went in and told Mother. At first she was quite angry, then she laughed and told him it was the right thing to do because she could get along without pots, but a soldier might not. Next time though, please ask.

Thursday, June 22, 1944

There was no Domestic Arts exam. Instead, the teacher made us cook a meatless but nutritious dinner *utilizing* wartime rations. Nancy and I cooked macaroni and cheese, and Nancy made a gravy to go over it.

"They do that in the army," she said. "Smother everything with gravy and that way no one can tell what's underneath." I made a salad because I knew how to do that from my own garden. We passed.

> *They had seen some time pass in this place and were telling us of all the many things the Germans did to the people around here which were terrible and unimaginable to believe.*

Friday, June 23, 1944
5:00 p.m., before the dance.

I am sitting here all dressed up ready for the dance. We got our marks back today and I passed everything, though my Math mark was a pretty close thing. I'm now officially done with elementary school.

We got out at noon so we could get ready for our graduation dance. First we get our graduation certificates in a ceremony, then the parents go home and we have our dance. I'm sitting very carefully in my dress because I don't want to get it creased. Mother knows I invited George to the dance. Here is how it happened:

Mother and Aunt Lily were fussing over me. Aunt Lily left work early "for the occasion," she said. She was putting on my lipstick.

"She's too young for lipstick," Mother protested.

"Oh, let the girl enjoy herself," Aunt Lily told her. "I picked this nice pink shade that's barely noticeable. Sit still, Bobby, or you're going to have lopsided lips."

My palms were sweating and my legs kept twitching. Mother still didn't know about George. What was I going to do!

"Bobby, do sit still," Aunt Lily said. Mother was tugging at my hair.

"I invited George from the hospital to go to the dance with me," I blurted out.

There was a big silence and I thought maybe they hadn't heard because Aunt Lily still held my chin, then I noticed she wasn't putting on lipstick, just staring at me. Mother suddenly tugged my hair so tight she pulled my eyes back until they were mere slits.

"You did what?" she said very quietly. (That's her worst mad voice, when she's quiet. I like her better yelling.)

"I invited George to come to the dance, but it's not a date. He knows I can't date until I'm sixteen. We're just going as friends," I told her.

"Well, you can just *un*-invite him," she said. "Imagine, taking a grown man to a child's dance." She gave my hair another hard tug. Tears filled my eyes.

"I can't," I said. "Besides, he's not that old and he's never been to a graduation dance. He said he's never been to anything normal for two years. It's why he got himself better, so he could go to the dance." At that moment nothing in the world was more important to me than George coming to the dance. Not even Mother's *towering rage.*

Mother let go of my hair. I moved the muscles around my eyes to make sure they weren't permanently stretched.

"Well, this is a fine time to tell me," she said.

"I tried to tell you earlier but I couldn't decide when was the right time and then, suddenly, it was the dance," I told her.

"This just beats all." Mother sat down on my bed. "He's probably up there getting ready right now." She was quiet a moment, then, "How's he getting here?"

"He said he'd take the hospital bus," I told her.

"The bus!" Mother exclaimed. She flew out of the room and I heard her dialling the phone.

"She's calling George to tell him not to come," I wailed to Aunt Lily.

"Don't be such a goose. She's phoning to tell him we'll pick him up in my car. He can't take a bus and walk all the way here when he's not been well," Aunt Lily said. "We're going to have a full car."

"What will Grandma say?" I asked.

"Tell you what," she said. "I'll ask my boyfriend, Sam, to come so Grandma won't know which one of us to be mad at."

The French have suffered plenty both through the destruction of their towns and the Germans' method which consists of loading themselves with loot from shops and homes before leaving and burning the place.

Friday, June 23, 1944

It's after midnight but I had to write about the dance. It was the grandest time I've ever had, yet at the same time the saddest. I can't stop crying. Here is how it happened:

Mother and Dad and I went to pick up George in Aunt Lily's car. At the hospital, my tongue suddenly wouldn't work. It flopped around in my mouth and I couldn't even talk to George. I'd never seen George in anything but a bathrobe or casual pants. He had on his uniform and he looked so handsome. I couldn't believe it. He gave me a corsage that Mother pinned on me. All the nurses were smiling at us. Alex was there and he touched my hand and said, "Have a good time at the dance. You too, George. And take care of my little sister." He almost sounded like Alex.

I heard Mother sniffling behind me and Dad said to her, "Don't go getting all weepy on me."

Back home Dad took a bunch of pictures of me and George. Brian made goofy faces at me the whole time to try and make me laugh. Even Caroline was there with little Billy to see us off.

Grandma didn't know who to ignore, George, or Aunt Lily's boyfriend, Sam, but I heard her tell Mother she would have another Caroline on her hands in no time. Dad's eyebrows drew down into one long black line hearing that, but Mother quickly said, "We certainly hope so. We're very proud of Caroline."

I don't know what Grandma thought of that.

Brian and Stephen walked to the school because we couldn't all fit in the car. I got my graduation certificate, then the parents went home and we went to the dance.

The gym had red, blue and white streamers all over it. It didn't look at all like the place we used to run sweaty circles around in gym class.

When George and I went up to the door, I suddenly had this horrible feeling I'd made a terrible mistake. Everyone was staring at us. Then the principal, Mr. Smith, came over and I thought he was going to kick George out. Instead, he said Mother had told him I'd brought a friend of mine and Alex's from the hospital, and he hoped George would have a nice time.

I still couldn't talk or even look at George without blushing. I didn't know how I'd get through the whole night silent and crimson.

"Which one is Betty?" George asked. "Which one causes the Worm of Jealousy to twist in your stomach." He was teasing me but it didn't hurt. In fact, it made me laugh and everything was fine after that.

It was a bit awkward at first dancing, but I just put one hand in George's and the other on his shoulder and it was fine.

Then Nancy and I jitterbugged together, though we didn't kick up too high because of our dresses! Then everyone gave it a try.

Dad picked us up at 11:00 p.m. and George walked me to the

door of our house while Dad waited in the car to take him back to the hospital. I knew Mother was on the other side of the door, though she didn't come out.

George took my hand. "I had a swell time," he said. "I meant to tell you all night how nice you look. Real nice. I knew yellow would suit you fine."

He looked at Dad sitting in the car, then back at me.

"I didn't want to tell you at the dance," he said. "But I'm being demobbed. I'm going home to Saskatchewan on Monday. I'll finish getting better, then the government's paying for me to go to school and learn a trade. The war should be over soon and everything's going to be different then. Really different."

George was going away.

"I'm hoping you'll write to me," he said, and he handed me a paper with his address. "I'll write back. I'm getting pretty good at writing with my left hand now. You might even be able to read it."

I know he was joking to make me feel better so I tried to smile, but from the look on his face, I don't think it worked.

"When your sixteenth birthday comes around, I'll be back here to take you on a proper date. That's a promise. If you want me to, that is. Just let me know if you don't and I'll understand."

He quickly kissed my cheek, then he was gone. I have a big, empty, hurting space inside now.

Saturday, June 25, 1944

I slept in until 11:00 a.m. Mother came in and brought me a cup of tea and sat on the side of the bed. "I'm sorry George is leaving," she said.

"He says he's coming back when I'm sixteen for a proper date," I told her.

"That would be nice," she said. "You never know what can happen. I've known your father since I was ten, not that we were going out or anything. Grandma wouldn't let me out of the house for a date until I was eighteen."

Then she held me real tight so I could cry.

This country here is certainly a German ravaged place—it will be a long time before it will return as ever before.

Sunday, June 26, 1944

Today is Alex's birthday. I asked Mother if I could go by myself to the hospital first before the rest of them. The hospital seemed really empty without George, even though there are still hundreds of men there.

Alex is walking much better so we went outside. He's more here than ever before. He asked me about Caroline's baby and was quite anxious about Brian, but I assured him Dad wouldn't let him go to war. Mother says the doctors told her Alex is making rapid progress and hopefully will be home by the end of July.

I finished reading the last entry in my diary to Alex, all about the dance and George going away. After I closed my old diary, I gave Alex his birthday gift—the real diary Mother had given me for Christmas, and the box Brian had made to put it in. Alex picked it up and flipped through the blank pages. "I remember how you like words," I told him.

His forehead puckered slightly, then he looked at me. Really looked at *ME!* For the first time, I believed Alex was truly back. He placed the diary in the box and we sat waiting for everyone else to come.

Sunday, June 27, 1944

I went over to Aunt Lily's this afternoon and took her to the back of the garden near the fence.

"The love-lies-bleeding is coming up again," I said, pointing at the plant starting to climb the fence. "I wasn't going to tell you because I know you didn't like it, because you thought it killed Uncle Billy." I wasn't explaining myself very well. "I really was going to pull it out, but I couldn't because it's alive."

Aunt Lily stared at the plant a while. "I know the plant didn't kill Billy," she said. "The war did that. You can leave it in. You've done a wonderful job of the garden. You must have a green thumb."

I never thought a lot about the war before. It was just something that was part of my life: uniforms downtown; no meat or sugar at times; the knitting club. But I think war is about fragments and pieces—bits of home, families, Alex's mind, George's body torn apart—and your heart breaking and your love lies bleeding. But Alex is getting better, Aunt Lily has Sam, and hopefully Caroline's James and Nancy's brother will come home safe. Come September I start high school, and in two years I have a date with George. I wonder if next spring the love-lies-bleeding will come up again. Probably.

> *If wishes were true, I should like to see the end of the war before January, be in England for a leave and be home by spring.*
>
> *From your son*

Promotion to buy Victory Bonds, Toronto 1942

appallingly

misery

wretched

glum

ambition

profusion

withering

forlorn

tantalizing

concoctions

enterprising

grimaced

philandering

latice

humiliated

perpetually

endurance

contrite

impeccable

mortified

capable

demurely

muffled

crestfallen

heart-rending

pityingly

humiliated

dire straits

gracious

unholy

incur

wrath

wretchedly

contortions

utilizing

towering rage

In order of appearance

Also by Barbara Haworth-Attard

Home Child

At first Matthew suggested getting a Home boy. But I said
"no" flat to that. "They may be all right—I'm not saying
they're not—but no London street Arabs for me," I said.
"Give me a native born at least. There'll be a risk, no matter who we get. But I'll feel easier in my mind and sleep
sounder at nights if we get a born Canadian."

Marilla Cuthbert
Anne of Green Gables © 1908

"Calf's dead." Mr. Wilson stomped into the kitchen
and kicked off his barn boots by the porch door.

Sadie took one look at her father's face, thundercloud black with anger, and hurriedly set a large bowl
of porridge on the table. She placed a small pitcher of
maple syrup next to it. Dad's *indulgence*, Mama called
it.

"Can't see any clear reason for it. Cow seemed
healthy throughout." He picked up the pitcher and
poured a steady stream of thick, brown liquid over the
porridge. Lucky thing, Sadie thought watching him,
that it had been a good year for maple syrup. Sunny
days and frosty nights had kept the sap flowing from
the maple trees in the back bush longer than usual this
past spring.

Sadie's mother turned from the stove carrying a